IN EXTREMIS
and Other Alaskan Stories

In Extremis
and Other Alaskan Stories

—————Jean Anderson—————

Plover Press
Kaneohe, Hawaii
1989

Printed and bound in the United States of America

Book Design: Roger Eggers
Cover Photography: Tom Anderson

Library of Congress Cataloging-in-Publication Data

Anderson, Jean, 1940–
    In extremis and other Alaskan stories.
    Contents: In extremis—Parting out—Into the heart
of winter—[etc.]
    1. Alaska—Fiction.   I. Title.
PS3551.N368I5 1989   813'.54   89-3507
    ISBN 0-917635-06-X
    ISBN 0-917635-07-8 (pbk.)

    The author would like to thank the Alaska State Council on the Arts for generous support in the form of an Individual Artist Fellowship, which freed time for the writing of several of these stories.
    The following stories have been published previously, some in slightly different form: "In Extremis" in *The Chariton Review*, Northeast Missouri State University (Fall 1986); "Into the Heart of Winter" in *Inroads: Alaska's Twenty-Seven Fellowship Writers*, Alaska State Council on the Arts, Anchorage, AK, 1988; "Vreelund" in *Alaska Quarterly Review*, University of Alaska Anchorage (Spring/Summer 1987); "Skin" in *Hunger and Dreams: the Alaskan Women's Anthology*, Fireweed Press, Fairbanks, AK, 1983; "Ruth" in *In the Dreamlight: Twenty-One Alaskan Writers*, Copper Canyon Press, Port Townsend, WA, 1984, and in *Heartland*, the Sunday supplement of the *Fairbanks Daily News-Miner*, June 23, 1985; and "Fixing Blame" in *Stories*, Boston, MA (Fall 1984).
    Grateful acknowledgement is made for permission to reprint portions of the following:

Joanne Townsend: Excerpt from "To Julie," *On a Bright Morning*, McKay Publishing Company, Anchorage. Copyright © 1988 by Joanne Townsend.

WB Music Corp.: Lyrics from "Swanee," Words by Irving Caesar, Music by George Gershwin. Copyright © 1919 by WB Music Corp. & Irving Caesar Music Corp. (Renewed.) All rights reserved. Used by permission.

Sierra Club: Excerpt from *Oil on Ice* by Tom Brown. Copyright © 1971 by the Sierra Club. All rights reserved.

Roberts Rinehart, Inc. Publishers, POB 3161 Boulder, Colorado 80303: Excerpt from *Bears of Alaska in Life & Legend* by Jeff Rennicke. Copyright © 1987 by Christina Watkins.

Little Brown and Company, 34 Beacon Street, Boston 02108: Excerpt from *Blue Highways, A Journey Into America* by William Least Heat Moon. Copyright © 1982 by William Least Heat Moon.

Distributed by
The Talman Company, Inc.
150 Fifth Avenue
New York, NY 10011

For my parents,
Blanche and Clifford Schulze

"And what I coaxed you 5000 miles
north of home to learn
was never weather but possibility. . . ."

Joanne Townsend, "To Julie,"
from *On a Bright Morning*

CONTENTS

IN EXTREMIS
and Other Alaskan Stories

In Extremis

"When environmentalists describe the arctic eco-system as 'fragile' or 'vulnerable,' the oilmen scoff. Their word for it is *hostile*. Either description fits."

Tom Brown, *Oil on Ice: Alaskan Wilderness at the Crossroads*

I'm not a ghoul. God knows, I am not a ghoul. But I've learned a few things by living.

For instance, most people have no sense of distance about life. No perspective. Myself included, some-times. That was what I was thinking, in fact, as the plane banked. It was 1976, and I'd already been work-ing on the Slope for eighteen months—seven-twelves for a month, then two weeks off, you know. Prudhoe Bay, Alaska's North Slope. But the sight of those oil rigs hunched like mosquitoes hitting a vein, the piss-colored upright, squat-looking biscuit-cutter storage tanks, and those crude metal buildings all spread out across the tundra in the middle of nowhere, with heavy equipment moving along like so many friggin' orange bugs— The whole damned train-layout delicacy of this vast, buzzing mechanized hellhole seen from the air—! Well, it was still something I could put in no perspective at all.

It's a living, I guess.

1

In Extremis

My dad used to say that about factory work when I was a kid growing up in Detroit. Him working the Ford assembly line—which, according to local legend in Detroit was supposed to be like going to heaven. Then, at least. In the late '40s and the '50s. But to Dad it was always his own little purchase on hell. A toehold, you know. Dad's purchase on hell, at Ford, buying us all a tract home and so forth. School clothes, food on the table, a used Ford station wagon of our own.

Well— My name's Len Peacock, don't you know. Leonard Martin Peacock Junior, and I guess I'm Dad's son to the core. I was thinking that too, anyway, that day in '76. And of her, the girl, Angie. And Christ-Almighty, if I wasn't reciting myself a poem to boot, as the jet engines roared and shimmied out noise and the air pressure pushed against my chest, descending. While the wheels began to toe the runway, I was saying to myself a poem by William Butler Yeats. Swilling the last of the Jack Daniels from one of those doll-baby bottles and reciting myself some Yeats, the poem's last lines:

> "Being so caught up,
> So mastered by the brute blood of the air,
> Did she put on his knowledge with his power
> Before the indifferent beak could let her drop?"

"Leda and the Swan." That's the title of it. Then we'd landed, and it was seven-twelves again. Just being there, you know; ordinary, everyday shit-eating—life with no perspective.

Except for the girl. Which was all in my head any-way—like Yeats' poem, for Chrissakes. And myself like Dad there too, poems.

2

You see, I don't know what it was about her, really. Her eyes maybe. They were deep-set, like Fran's, my wife's, but another color. Icy blue, like lake water could be some days. This pale vertiginous God-damned color shot through with washed-out gray—like Lake Erie or St. Clair in a winter storm. Christ, they were holy-looking eyes, almost transfigured looking, with that sad, scalded purity of icy lake water just the hour or so after the worst kind of storm.

It was May, I think—May in the real world, though it was still winter up there on the Slope. But with daylight. Snow melted a bit, then frozen into dirty dry waves like some God-forsaken sea. I had it all worked out, how I'd saunter up to her desk still feeling my Jack Daniels and all and strike up this serious conversation about those photocopies.

But the wall was bare, you see, when I got there— no photocopies.

Well, I'm getting ahead of myself. She'd worked there for six months or so, just the length of time Fran and I had been separated. We still slept together sometimes, Fran and I, when I came in to Fairbanks for R'n'R. That's what it was called, the two weeks off, what we all called it. R'n'R. Like Vietnam, which isn't so far-fetched a similarity as you might think.

Anyhow, I'd go pick the kids up to take 'em to a movie, lunch, whatever—Jeff eight then and Tabsy five and the old Lacey Street Theater still open. So— So, we'd eat at Co-Op, hamburgers and fries and chocolate shakes all around, then go to our movie. And, some-times, when we'd get back, there'd be Fran, watching TV and sipping her damned diet Coke and wearing some filmy nighty or other.

3

Well— Anyway, we were not divorced. And I always had this, this feeling that the kids—approved. Without really knowing anything, if you see what I mean. Seemed—more or less natural.

It was my working on the slope that had done it to us, I thought then. Screwed us. Still do, essentially, I guess. My being gone so much, I mean. But I guess it was something more than that all along, like Fran bitching to me about the money—real big money—how it didn't mean *anything* when it was costing us our life. And me thinking about—well, the way the girl, Angie, could stay in my mind. Angie.

I'd heard other people call her Angie. And I'd seen the photocopies. These weird—*things* she had taped up on the wall behind her desk. Photocopied bits of the girl who'd worked there before her, you see. That's what they were. An elbow, then this long straight hair spread like a fan. You know—like, this other girl's left cheek pushed up against the glass of the machine to make this flat, black and white—*thing*. The side of her lips, a few teeth maybe, a hint of eyelashes—God.

Not pictures at all but these ghastly, ghost-eaten bits and pieces of this other girl.

Who'd cracked up, they said. The isolation, possibly, although I personally attributed it to drugs. Or tried to in my own mind anyhow. Then.

Because the thing of it was that I was thinking—or feeling, maybe—that nothing could matter anyway. That working up here was such a hellhole situation because that's what life really was anyway. For everybody. If they'd just wise up enough to see it. Or admit it. Whatever—

As if my unhappiness was some kind of wisdom, you see. So that I felt as if I finally understood those

4

photocopies. And why she'd left them up there, scotchtaped to the wall above her desk. Because I assumed the other girl must have originally taped 'em. Must've put 'em up on the wall before she cracked—or during, whatever.

I thought I could talk to her about how I understood, now, why she'd left 'em up there and all. Because she hadn't *known* the other girl, she'd just been hired to replace her.

So, anyway, landing in the plane, I'd been working it all out in my mind, perspective and all, so that everything had come to focus on Angie. On her eyes and her skin and this dark honey color of her hair. And on the way she moved her hand sometimes, holding out a requisition form or passing me a key to the chefs' pantry. She'd push that brass key across the blotting pad on her desk with that narrow, pale, flat little wrist turning in a delicate, slow arc so that the fine blue veins glinted at me suddenly then disappeared, like a fish in water.

I thought I could—make contact with her, let's say, by approaching on the subject of those photocopies. It was not just sex.

But, sure as hell, the day I got back—an afternoon about 3:00, still her duty hours—they were all gone. No photocopies. The wall was bare. She wasn't even *there*, for Chrissakes, and God if my heart didn't stop for several beats. It was like—well, like *everything* had come to depend on her being there, you see. Almost like I was drowning when she *wasn't*, my whole damned life sort of flashing before me, how I was this club-footed loser who'd kidded himself his whole damned life about everything, even about Fran and the kids.

In Extremis

You see, I have a clubfoot. That's why I read, I guess, aside from Dad; why I became a cook, a chef, in the first place. When I was born with it, Dad out and refused. He would not have it operated. He would not, he said, have something that might keep me out of the factory taken away from me. So, you know, I've never worked in a factory, never gone to war—just the age for Vietnam, too—and always been, instead, sort of on the edge of things, on the fringe.

Except—well, I happen to be tall and "a looker," that's what Fran says anyhow, and I've never gotten on badly with girls or women—or even with other men, you see. My being a loser was all about something else, I was thinking. Not my foot at all, but my not taking hold—about my accepting a purchase on hell, just as Dad had done. A loser— Chasing, like a fool, after some young girl I'd never even spoken more than twenty-five or thirty words to in six damned months.

But then there she was, just sauntering down the hall. Not sauntering exactly, because there was always such a sadness to her. But she was walking slow-as-you-please down the hallway as if I wasn't right there drowning.

Even her walk, that sauntering—took my breath away. And not just sex.

It was a trailer, you see, the clerks' building, with these narrow, dark hallways carpeted in this moss-colored indoor-outdoor carpeting that eats up light, and her skin just glowed in all that dark. God, how I had the hots for her then, trying to hide it. But, like I said, more than that too. Like some damned obsession.

6

"Key to the chefs'—?" That's what she was saying,
for God if they don't keep everything under lock'n'key
up there on the Slope, even the supply requisition forms
locked up tight as the chefs' pantry, with those little
clerks holding all the keys—

And she was talking in that detached, cool high-
pitched little voice of hers, just as if she couldn't see
how my heart was flipping and flopping inside me—

"Yeah. That too," I said, and she turned those amaz-
ing eyes up to look at me.

I wanted to say I love you. Then, already, never
even having truly *spoken* to her. But instead, like a
fool and a loser, I cleared my throat. Real hard. Then
I said, "There's 'True Grit' showing as the movie tonight. Ah—you know, John Wayne as that drunken
ol' Rooster Cogburn—? Thought I might—"

And she was grinning. Actually that, a sweet, kindly
little grin. "Oh, Leonard," she said, "I can't." She didn't
say anything for a minute or so, then, "Sorry," she
said, "thanks anyway." And her eyes were sad and
scalded again.

I was hired as a baker, you see, though my training
is more along the usual chef's lines. And I do love
cooking and baking, am damned good at it. So, going
to a movie in the evening would have been the last
thing I'd need, really—having to start in baking at 4:00
A.M. as usual, which she knew. She might have thought
my asking her was something of—well, something of
a sacrifice, I guess. Or maybe I looked hurt, frowned—
something. Maybe she even thought of my foot, how,
because of it, I probably have no luck with women—
which they all seem to think, usually, so that it—my
foot—as my friend Walt, in high school, always used

7

to say as his joke—actually gives me "a leg up." My foot—

Because she was talking again, in that cool, whispery little voice, almost apologizing. "I just don't like staying up late. Nothing personal. But—I've got a little wine. I get off at seven. And—and if you'd like to come by my room at about seven-thirty— Well, maybe we could listen to some music, some tapes for a while—"

She had *no* reputation. I mean, I'd have bet anybody any amount that she'd had nothing going with any other male, or female, up there in six months, because I'd had my ears open, you see. Though not in the crude way that sounds—because the way I wanted her was entirely different than anything I can remember feeling before— And—well, anyway, it's just the truth that up there, on the Slope, they all have reputations. Labels. Females do, in a week or a month's time. Puts out, hates men, a tease, whatever. But not her. Strange—slightly strange. Terra incognita. That was the only one she had. Only label, and it fascinated me too.

Not just because she was so beautiful. But something about the true self of her, if you see what I mean. Unknown, maybe a bit strange— And again, I am *not* a ghoul. No. Like the way my becoming a chef must have seemed to Dad—poetic, a bit marvelous. Or like coming North had felt to me at first. Something pure and different and rare and—and really *right*. I'd felt that way, at one time, about marrying Fran, in fact—and I was feeling that way again now, all tensed up inside and ready for something. Something that mattered.

"Sure," I said, maybe talking too quickly. "Sure. That'd be—I mean, I'd—yeah. Great. Sure. I'll be there." She was almost laughing, only time I'd ever seen her do that. I had to double back, in fact, to find out for certain where her room was— though I must admit I had a pretty good guess. But I was that flustered. "Seven-thirty," I said, backing off down the hallway. "I'll be there."

Well— Her room was in another trailer, clerks' housing. She had the door slightly ajar. The lights were off and she had three or four of those little church candles lit, sitting atop the shelf and the nightstand and one there next to the upholstered chair that all the rooms have. They were in little red, jeweled-looking glass cups, and they cast a red glow around her room that made me think of church, though I guess that's probably not the effect she was after.

She'd come to the door to let me in, and right away I could smell the pot. I mean, even if I hadn't noticed the dreamy way she was moving. What I thought was that she must be afraid. She must be *that* afraid that she'd already got herself a little high—and I'd have to catch up. If I could—

She sat me in the chair, and she began loading up the tape player. These Beatles tunes, though my thought was that she was too young to be that onto them. She was holding her maryjane out in one hand beside her while she fiddled through the tapes—we'd hardly even said that many words, you know—and then she just handed it toward me—her cigarette—and began to talk.

"My parents died when I was fifteen," she said. The Beatles were singing away—"Eleanor Rigby," I think it was—and she sorta leaned back on her bed and just started right in talking. Not even calling forth my spec-

9

ulations about the damned photocopies. "Automobile accident," she said.

I answered some or other polite thing, and she was going on, as if whatever I might say could make no difference. As if she'd already made her mind up to—to confide in me, open up to me, I guess.

"The strange thing, Leonard—"

"Call me Len," I said, but she didn't.

"The strange thing was that I wasn't that torn up by it. I was an only child—but there were my grandparents, my mother's parents, who were still young, and I moved in with them. We'd cry together, nights, for quite a while, but then, after a time, it was—normal. As if nothing that terrible had happened after all. The world was not changed. And I could feel—certain advantages. Cruel as that sounds."

I was nodding like a fool, puffing at her cigarette—which was damned weak—saying my "Um—"

"My grandparents were—tired of childrearing, I guess, and my parents had left a trust fund for me. And, well, I seemed to have lots of freedom. I mean, my grandparents loved me, and I them. And my parents—the same. But beyond that, my grandparents trusted me. There was no—hovering. When I was 17, I said I'd like to go to Europe—for a summer, you know. With two friends. And they approved, which my parents—probably—would never have done."

I sat there sucking away on the cigarette, more or less in an emotional stupor. Amazed, I guess, that this beautiful girl who'd held me in thrall for weeks had, apparently, accepted me. Was leveling with me. That she had a personal life—she was more than this figment of my mind—and she was sharing her interpretation of her life with me. It was intimacy—what I'd dreamed

10

of, corny as that sounds—even that she could lie back on her bed and talk while the church lights glowed and flickered and wafted nice perfume all around us, and—God!—I was in as much of a rosy glow as the room, even without the weed.

Anyway, my side of the conversation at this point—which I can't call to mind just now—really amounted to nothing but polite noises. She kept on talking, real quiet and polite too, but hell-bent, you know. As if it was a now-or-never type thing. Confession time, was what I was thinking, and I loved it.

"Rosa and Elaine and I went to London, through the English countryside, and across the Channel to France, then on by rail to Paris. And it was beautiful, Leonard. *Beautiful*— I wouldn't turn 18 until fall, but I felt—oh—*myself*. There, that summer in Paris, I felt more mature and secure and certain about who I was and why I was alive than I'd ever felt before. Or than I have since."

I'd felt that way about that age, reading. Odd as that sounds. Dad's son, as I said, though he even tried to write. But I didn't want to say all that to her. I can't even talk that well, you know, and lots of the stuff I read was trash. But I knew what she meant.

She was sitting up on her bed now, and she extended that pale right arm so that I passed her what was left of the cigarette. She puffed on it again before she talked.

"It happened in Paris," she said, and at first I thought she was continuing about finding herself and so on. But she wasn't.

"Rosa and Elaine decided to go on to Brussels, but I didn't want to leave. I'd fallen in love with Paris, I think, and I wanted to stay there as long as I could. Even if it meant staying on alone. We'd been staying

11

in a youth hostel, and—well, it was safe enough, I thought. It *was*, in fact. It was a nice, clean, inexpensive place. And—despite the fact of my parents' death—I was innocent, I suppose. Besides, I'd begun to fall in love with Paris, as I said, and the whole world seemed magical, and *safe*. Wondrous and beautiful and—and *my* oyster, you see? We all thought it would be safe—be *fine*—for me to stay on alone.

"They'd come back in four days, and we'd retrace our steps and head home to Ithaca. I was raised in Ithaca, New York, you see, which seems two worlds away by now. And—and I could spend all the time I'd like in the Louvre and walking along the Seine— Which I did."

She stopped at this point and motioned to me, by patting the mattress, that I should come and sit beside her. Which—of course—I did. Though I was beginning to feel—well, eerie, I guess. It was something in the air, I think. A mood emanating from the girl. From Angie.

Anyway, I sat beside her, she with her legs tucked up under her and her left arm trailing across the bed toward me, while she continued with this story of hers.

Not a story—I mean, her *life*. I mean, I *did* believe it, and still do.

Anyhow, possibly because I was nearer to her now, or maybe because of the marijuana, her voice had grown even softer. Really soft.

"It happened as I was walking along the Seine, the second day I was alone. It was afternoon, and—and I'd stopped walking at a spot where views were—fabulous, really fine, Leonard—in three directions. I was just—oh—star-struck, I guess, more or less, by the beauty. And, and—this cab stopped. A Paris city cab,

12

but driven by a tall, blonde young man who spoke no English.''

For the minute, I could identify with this guy, still saying my "Um—''

"No English at all. And very little French, either, because I spoke some French. I'm not sure what language he spoke, though I've guessed at Finnish. Norwegian, maybe. Anyway, he wanted me to get into the cab. And he was so—so beautiful, so incredibly handsome, Leonard. And I got in, and he drove away, with me sitting in front, beside him, like a princess carried off on a stallion by a prince. I mean, that's exactly how it felt, at first— But then he was—''

She stopped now, crushing the butt of the cigarette in an ashtray and closing her eyes, which hardly anybody does with pot, as you probably know. Fiddling her fingers through her hair for a bit. Not talking. I didn't say a word either.

"He raped me,'' she said suddenly. "He drove to an alley somewhere in Paris and raped me. I fought—I mean, this beautiful-looking boy—and I'd had no experience—and he raped me, pushed me out of the taxi when he was done with me, and drove away. Neither of us ever able to exchange a word that made sense— I—I— It almost made me—insane.

"It did, in fact. I stayed in Paris. I wanted it that way, though my grandparents came— And I would have had the baby in Paris, in a—in an old-fashioned home for unwed young women. But I miscarried. Then I came home to Ithaca.

"But the worst thing of it was— Well, no, no. It was all awful, from the start.'' She was shaking her head. "It was—well, *all* the things my parents' death might have been but had not. It was—*hell*, Leonard. It was hell."

I was patting her shoulder by now, trying to find something or other to say.

"For a year after that, I—I drifted in and out of madness. That's how it seemed, drifting. Most of it I can't even remember now."

"Well, that's *good*," I said, beginning to rub her back. "You don't want to remember it—"

"Oh, but I *do* remember one thing," she said. "The thing that made me go mad. I do remember that."

I didn't think I wanted to hear it, but what could I say? I mean, I'm no ghoul, yet till then I'd loved her. I said nothing, kept rubbing her back.

"I remember what I thought—while he was raping me." She was whispering now. Truly whispering, her eyes closed. "I'll never be able to forget what I thought—then."

Again I said nothing. Rubbed her back, gently as I could. As I say, maybe I still loved her, I wasn't sure anymore, but God, I was beginning to wish I could—could just *leave*—anything, *escape*, you know? I repeat, I am *not* a ghoul. But I said nothing.

"I've never told anyone," she said. "I've never found anyone I thought I could tell."

My hands had stopped moving on her back by then. Just stopped. "Go ahead," I said. God knows why I said it, because the majority portion of my self actually did *not* want to know this terrible thing. But— Well, I guess I'd already loved her that many weeks. It seemed like I'd been born to love her—the way this Finnish kid, or whatever he was, had been born, you see, to— Christ! Creepy as it sounds, that's what I was thinking, anyway. Like it was some fate or other to hear this

14

tale of her life from her, you see. That maybe this was the form my love had to take.

Anyway, I thought she needed to tell it. "It's alright," I said in this wimpy voice, giving up on the backrub and just deciding I'd be there. What the hell. Sorta tucking both my hands between my thighs and sitting silently again.

Though a part of me, weird as it sounds, loved her even more by now.

She opened her eyes again, tears in them but not falling. The tears made that blue color look even more scalded. "Leonard," she said, "thank you. What I thought— Well— I thought—" She closed her eyes, opened them. "I thought that I had seen the face of God."

Her hands were over her face by then. She was weeping into them, the tears sliding through her fingers and running down her wrists toward those blue veins.

For a second or two, I just sat there. What can you say to somebody else's—words? Worse than the ache in some poem. Somebody's hell-holy non sequitur that's hanging in the air like revealed truth? The face of God—

I mean, it was *true*, I guess. It was true enough for her, anyways—

And in an odd way, I even thought I knew what she meant. Then. As if, much as she hated what was happening, this brutality was her fate. Something like that. This was the high point in her life somehow, maybe. That's what I thought then, anyhow, that night in her room. That she'd—well, just *known* everything would be downhill after. Changed. Everything would *be* "after."

As if, in this—this un-Christly, God-damned *horror*, she'd made some kind of contact with—with— Well, shit. With something ultimate, if you see what I mean, and she could not accept it, after.

I'd had friends tell me that kind of thing about war. About Vietnam, killing or nearly being killed there. And my old buddy Walt Reyman—best friend I ever had, him with his "leg up" business—Walt, Walt. Well, he used to say it all the time. In different words, of course, and less awful. But about stock cars, before one of the damned things got him, at 19.

Well— For me, the odd thing was that I *still* loved her—maybe even more than before. But in an entirely different way now. Maybe the way I'd loved Walt. I no longer loved her like a woman. I no longer wanted her—

I sort of— Well, I leaned over and patted her hand. She'd taken her hands from her face by now and was, well, like—drying them on her slacks. Rubbing the backs and the palms on the fabric of her slacks, trying to calm her face. So, I took up her left hand and patted it very gently. That was what I did, you see.

She turned her eyes toward mine and looked at me— God, such a look. And I wanted to say it then, again. Suddenly. Just as before, I wanted to say I love you.

But I *couldn't*, you see. Because of what all she'd said and been through. And because— Because I loved her in so many different ways by now. In such entirely changed and strange ways. Which were—foreign to me, you see. And I am not a ghoul. But I loved her.

I closed my eyes for a second, took a real deep breath. "Well—you go on, don't you?" That's what I said instead of I love you, hardest thing I've ever done. And she nodded, looked in my eyes real slow, then looked away.

By the time she'd done that, it had all come back—the hots, the old simpler way of loving her, like a great ache, awful, so that I loved her now in so God-damned many ways, all of a sudden, I felt like I'd explode.

But of course I couldn't touch her then either, you see. Or say a word.

I couldn't. Because I suddenly just *knew*— Something. Something about myself, and about her.

What kind of people we both were.

Are. What kind of people.

Not lovers.

"Yes," she said, real slow. "Yes. You go on—"

I—I—I kissed her hands. Just that. Real gently, you know? Then I stood up, nodded good evening, and went back to my own room. No supper, nothing—Went to bed, got up the next A.M. at 3:00, same as always, and baked all day. Then—that afternoon—I turned in my pink slip. Decided it was time to drag up. Quit on 'em, I mean, without ever talking to Angie again. Ever. Not even telling her goodbye.

It was just—well, as I said, I knew what kind of person I was then. Perspective. Permanent.

I went back to Fran, patched things up, got a job right off as a chef in Fairbanks, and started honing in on my own life.

Been real happy since then, Fran and me and the kids. That's the oddest thing of all, because—well, I say it for the last time, I am *not* a ghoul. But, it was only after that, only after that one night spent staring into Angie's scalded eyes—only then, you see, that I really began to be happy.

17

Parting Out

"He found *us*," Dave says. Which is true, though I'm inclined to dispute it anyway. " '73. '74 was the year your Uncle Andrew died."

My husband and I sit at the breakfast table. We're watching a sliver of moon drift between slate-colored clouds, eating in semi-darkness as we always do on Saturday mornings in winter, but with light from the Christmas tree filtering in from the living room and the snowy stand of aspens beyond the dining room window beginning to glow in the first rays of morning light. People are swapping and selling on the radio behind Dave's shoulder—which I hate, "Tradeo"—and Dave has his scrap of paper and pencil ready, hoping for a spare wheel for the truck, while for some reason or other we've begun talking about birthdays. Our daughter, our youngest child, turned eighteen less than a month ago, yet the birth date we've focused on is the cat's.

"It had to be '74 that we found him—" I've just said, which brought on Dave's comment about my uncle's death.

That thought has silenced both of us—though not the swappers and sellers, someone with a playpen just now—the way suicide tends to do. My Uncle Andrew was a lawyer, a bachelor in his late sixties in 1974; my mother's older brother, a homosexual, and the only male in my family who entered a profession rather than business or a trade. My mother says it's true that he died with the revolver he'd kept beside his bed for years jammed between his lips.

"I guess you're right," I say. It must have been '73 that Nubbin, the cat, a scrawny kitten then, crawled up under the frame of the truck when we were spending a few days down the Kenai Peninsula in Seward, and adopted us. We brought him back to Fairbanks planning to turn him over to Pet Pride. But we thought he was a she at the time; and I'm trying to imagine the feel of gunmetal on my tongue, though I can't even begin to think of the rest of it.

"Nearly fifteen years—" I say, sighing out loud while I lift the coffee pot and pour, and Dave grabs his pencil to jot a phone number—somebody parting out a '78 Ford van.

Dave is in love. That's what I'm really thinking about. I've watched him every morning this week, and last week too, doing push-ups and knee bends on the floor next to the bed for half an hour in the darkness while he thinks I'm still asleep. I've watched him combing the thin strands of hair forward, then to the side, spreading them carefully with his fingers, patting at them, his eyes in the mirror bright with all this. I've watched him unfolding sweaters from the drawer—V-neck sweaters I bought for him that he never would wear before—then holding them up against his shirt-front to check for colors in the mirror. I know all the symptoms. Dave is in love.

A new student, I'm thinking. Or maybe a new faculty member. It's happened before, in a way, though this time it seems serious.

Parting Out

The sliver of moon, in a color that makes me think of a satin nighty, has disappeared into the dark center of the clouds, and I'm thinking of the girl's body— long and thin and pale maybe, the skin delicate and young, almost translucent, like our daughter's skin. Not a wrinkle anyplace or a wobbly bulge of flesh. Not a pockmark anywhere on her. Her hair might be blonde, an ash-colored sleekness to it—straight and long. Or maybe it's dark, nearly black, her eyes like coals that glow in that dusky face and her skin a color dark as the coffee I'm thickening up with Carnation, stirring to get exactly the right shade.

Maybe she has small breasts like his mother had, something Dave's always admired, not the full pen- dulous ones that run in my family. And her teeth are very small and neat, not wide like mine or long like Dave's. She must be a beauty—

Dave's stood up and gone to the phone, turned on the light to dial some number. Hers—? "A '78, you say?" He's holding his hand over the receiver while he clears his throat. "What I'm looking for is a fifteen- inch Ford wheel for a half-ton truck."

I'm too busy imagining her to listen to the rest of it, details of the other man's parting out. Her breath is probably very sweet, and she keeps her eyelids low over her eyes whenever she talks to Dave. She doesn't bat her eyes; she's too beautiful for that. After a lec- ture—the Civil War, maybe—she waits for him at the back of the classroom, fumbling with her stack of books, grabbing the stack up hastily when she sees that he's strapped up his books and the rest of it, those dog- eared photocopies he carries and his yellow legal pad— he writes his lectures on those yellow pads, with black Pentel pens that I buy for him at Pay 'n Save, circling

21

important points with green Pentel— Red is for grading papers—

Well, when she sees that he's stuffed all this into the black leather briefcase I got him for Christmas last year, on sale at Hops Stationery—what does she say to him? Something about Sherman's March to the Sea? There's summer in her voice, of course—

Dave's hung up the phone and moved down the hall to the bathroom. I can hear him brushing his teeth, that gargling noise he's been making for the past couple of weeks, since he's been in love. Maybe she wears bunny boots. Some of them still do that, beautiful big girls like Vikings, who smell of woodsmoke and pot and dogs. Girls who build their own cabins, haul their own water, and drive tiny Toyota trucks from which they emerge like disguised goddesses, like beautiful Keystone Cops climbing out of those tiny cars so gracefully despite everything, swathed in thick layers of Thinsulate and handspun wool—dogs' hair maybe. A girl like Venus emerging from her shell, leading with those huge dirty-white boots.

"I'm going over to take a look at the wheels this guy has," Dave is saying, while he pulls his parka out of the hall closet, gives it a shake. I'm nodding, sipping the dusky girl's skin, holding Nubbin on my lap. He'll stop by her place later, of course—a tiny apartment on campus with those glass bottles with cork lids that young women use to store things—noodles, flour, coffee—all glittering in the morning light on the kitchen counter. She's still in her bathrobe too, of course, as I am, but it's a plaid bathrobe, which she can get away with because she's so young, so beautiful—

"—noon or so," Dave is saying, and I'm nodding, lifting one hand to wave back. Does she call him Doctor Sanfield? Dave? Darling—?

"What—?" Dave's asking. He's eager to get out the door.

"—that party for Warren," I'm saying, God knows why. "Don't you remember it? At the Pump House? '79 or so?"

"No," Dave says, " 'fraid not. I've got to get this car started, Virginia." When he calls me Virginia, he's run out of patience.

The woman I'm thinking of was at Warren Foster's party—a birthday party. She was a bit younger than I am now probably, eight or ten years ago. She was dressed for success, in this silky cream-colored blouse and a dark tie-like thing, with a muted paisley skirt and a velveteen jacket. Permed hair. Though I'd never seen her before, or at least never spoken to her before—because in Fairbanks it does seem as if you've seen everybody someplace, at least once, before—she was telling me about how *un*conventional she was. She stressed the word that way, all the weight on the first syllable. How she'd come to Alaska on her own, after "a messy divorce," and how her children wished she'd be "more conventional." She was shaking her head to say all this, holding her head with a certain set to it, and I was thinking that she was old already (which I don't feel now myself—old, I mean, despite this new girl of Dave's—and despite the fact I'm already at an age probably a year or two past whatever her age was then, this *un*—). I was thinking that surely nobody cared anymore anyway, once a person reached a certain age, whether or not she was "conventional." And surely she *was* conventional enough—look how she's dressed, for God's sake!—and *did* children ever think such things about parents? Surely not—Uncle Andrew was a homosexual, for instance, and yet he was one of the most *conventional* persons—in all other ways except his death—I've ever known; he'd *never* leave his apartment without a suit jacket, and he drove only late-model American sedans, black Buicks or Oldsmobiles—

And as this woman talked, on and on it seemed, about what a disappointment—or a shock, perhaps—she was proving to be to her children, I was trying to keep my face straight, free of my thoughts, at least; trying to smile but not laugh; thinking how odd it was that I'd lived for fifteen years in Alaska and was still not truly an *un* either, though some of the others here were, in a way—like Warren himself maybe, whose birthday cake, finally, just read "Happy Birthday to Warren," though we'd joked about things it might say while chipping in for it. Like "Happy Birthday Old Foster," since he was sensitive about the fact that he was turning fifty, or—from the social worker in the group—"Happy Birthday Self-Actualized Foster," which I'd loved and wanted to have put on the cake, though no one else agreed.

"They'd be far happier if I'd just settle down and be like other parents," the woman said, giving her head that conventional shake again.

"They'll get over it," I answered, which was apparently the wrong thing to say, because she was frowning a little, trying not to. In a way I'm not conventional either. That's what I was thinking. I was born this way. I usually say the wrong thing, for instance, and my mind never will stay on the track. And look at me now, sitting here on the couch as if I had not a care in the world, while my husband of twenty-four years heads off for some secret tryst—

And I'm thinking of Warren Foster, how heavy he was at fifty, how much a failure in a way—though he had a Ph.D. How he never could keep his mind on track either; how he'd given up the chairmanship of his department at the school he'd taught in before in Michigan to come to Alaska, "God knows why," as he always put it; and how his kinky yellowish-gray hair would fly up whenever he turned his head—as he was always prone to do during any conversation; mid-sentence during one of his own sentences even—glancing or staring at something that set him off on a whole new topic. Yet, how charming that had been, in its way.

How he'd blushed over the cake, clapping his plump hands, looking as if he might cry, and how surprised he'd been—all of us, middle-aged and laughing, clapping and shouting when he came in the door; all yelling, "Happy Birthday, Warren!" like nine-year-olds in a private living room instead of gray-haired persons elbowing one another to fit around the table in one of the town's best restaurants.

But *Fairbanks*, after all, "where anybody can do almost anything with impunity; that's the charm of the place." Warren Foster said that to me once, a few months before he headed South again. And I agreed that it was true, though the thought crossed my mind when he said it that we only rarely *did* do anything out of the ordinary, any of us.

At his birthday party, I kissed Warren Foster on the lips while his live-in talked to a man with a beard, a man I'd truly never seen before, though he looked like a twin to dozens of others I had seen.

25

Parting Out

"Happy Birthday, Warren!"

I'm sure the girl must be tall. Maybe I'll get to see her. Maybe I'll follow Dave in the station wagon and peer in a window at them—sitting cross-legged—partly undressed maybe—on the floor on a woven rug in front of her woodstove, holding hands, nibbling one another's ears, there in a tiny cabin perched high on a snowy hilltop.

I carry Nubbin to the picture window, which looks straight south, toward the Alaska Range. The sun hasn't risen yet, but purple daylight is flooding the world, and Fairbanks lies stretched like a beautiful thick necklace, its colors like Christmas lights spread out before the peaks of the Range, which stretches above and beyond town in dark silhouette. Nearer to home, I can see large white snowy patches among the spruce trees, which are frozen fields, then birch woods, our easement, the highway, the lights of an occasional nearby house.

It's incredibly beautiful, a twilit winter beauty that I'm blessed to see nearly every winter morning and evening. And, of course, winters in Fairbanks last for seven months. I'm not sure what I feel about the girl—or Dave, his face tender again as it used to be for me. Years ago. Seeing a glimmer through the trees, I pick out the four new lights the highway department installed a week or so ago at the base of the road, a mile downhill. When you're going downhill, the road seems to head east through the woods, then straight south, exactly south, like the point of a compass. But, staring at the lights, I can see that the road at that point, at its very end or beginning—there where it meets the highway—really runs west, due west, or south-by-southwest maybe. Not simply south at all.

Into the
Heart of Winter

"In Medieval Europe it was thought that hibernating bears gave birth to shapeless lumps of flesh and licked them into bear cubs through the long winter nights."

Jeff Rennicke, *Bears of Alaska in Life & Legend*

Snow at the window, moon, fluorescence, snow.
Leslie's parents are arriving at the bus station—
Only it's not the bus station but the train station, for there's no bus station in Fairbanks, just the unlit and rutted parking lot of Oxford Assaying and Refining, a dealer in gold and other fine metals that sits downtown in a big beige box of a building made not of ice blocks but of plexiglass, cement squares, and linked chunks of plastic-coated steel.

Snow, and her parents are arriving at the train station (which is clean and modern, well-lit) but they've taken the Yukon Stage Line, coming from Cleveland by bus, traveling slowly but at great speed over miles and miles of almost identical highways, gliding across the hills and valleys and flat green plains, through all the rain and sunshine and sleet that fills North America, coming from Cleveland to Leslie into this blizzard.

27

And they each carry a rumpled paper sack: "Stuegers can't go anywhere without a paper sack," Dad's old joke—though of course Stuegers never do go anywhere.

Fluorescent snow ticking the window, and moon.

Moonlit snow makes dreams; Leslie believes this: her Polish grandmother in heaven is shaking a featherbed: bits of goose down, bits of cloud that fall slowly from the sky like tufts of sleep.

New sleep, dreams, yes, this snow at the window—

But her parents are arriving here from Cleveland, and the snowflakes fall on their foreheads and shoulders like kisses. They have never traveled anywhere (well, to Baltimore once, and Dad to Wisconsin in the CCC's, which no one was to speak of, ever, because, though he loved it, it carried the taint of poverty, even the memory, even the spoken sound) and they—her parents—must be covered in their journey with soft, soft kisses.

Snow, snow, fluorescent snow everywhere, and time: yes, her parents have broken time to travel here, into the heart of winter, to arrive by bus from Cleveland at the Fairbanks train station.

And her grown nieces, Mitzy and Rose, hold their grandparents' hands to form a chain; a simple chain of human faith and courage (courage needed in this tremendous journey) and the feathery snowflakes fall on all the plump shoulders like kisses—

Leslie has awakened in the hospital bed to distance.

She has not given birth again, but rolled the car, rolling and rolling the car into her own birth, it seems:

she is alive, her head rich with the rolling; the car her spaceship, her bus; the snow her own fluffed-up blanket; and the tundra beneath it even more cushiony than any featherbed—her own Mother Tundra.

Distance, moon, snow, and Leslie's parents are arriving from Ohio when she runs to greet them, running with no limp. They are all young, herself and her parents—plump, cheerful, young, weeping, the snowflakes falling on all the foreheads, covering all the lenses of all the glasses like fog, but not enough to mar this knowledge of kisses; of tears and hugs and caresses tender as falling snow—

And turkeys.

Yes, yes, turkeys. She read it once in a newspaper, in the *Daily News-Miner* in Fairbanks, Alaska, how the old sourdough, when his brother came for the first time (the only time) to his mining claim which still sits there on a hill outside Tanana—Tanana the Indian city—to his cozy hovel of log-cabin hut and mine—(a hand-dug mine that tunnels, dark, dark into the hill—) how he baked six turkeys.

How, when his brother came (alone, by bus, surely by bus, as the old and poor of all the world still surely travel, by bus—though even a car or a plane would be cheaper—or a spaceship—and faster—) by bus, coming from Pittsburgh, coming for the first time to Alaska (the *only* time), the two elderly brothers who had not touched flesh of their flesh for forty-one years—yes, he baked six turkeys.

Snow is falling everywhere in Fairbanks in March, though last week it was sunshine and 47 degrees, and the snowflakes are kisses too, and Leslie will rise from her hospital bed to bake one turkey.

She has no scratch anywhere on her body, only an ache in her head, in her heart, the ache of loving maybe, not the ache of living after rolling and rolling on Mother Tundra into this birth, but the ache of being given back all this love.

"I know, I know—" says Suzanne, Leslie's neighbor, sitting beside Leslie's bed. "I felt it too—*Yes*."

When Suzanne's plane, in midair, hit the other plane (like a miracle of hitting: Dad's boyhood vision, that two bullets, in midair, might hit, hit, hit—) Suzanne says that she thought, hitting, only of her parents.

Who live in upstate New York, but not together: not legally apart either; her parents: her dear dear mother, though of Dutch ancestry, being almost an American Indian healer, an anthropologist, though also then almost ordained as an Episcopal clergyperson; and her father—well—a man she has loved all her life in the way that you love *mysteries*.

In the way that you love hard old things—difficult and intricate; too firm-minded, perhaps; too hard-edged and whiskery to be as simple as he is in some things and too intelligent; too rigid; too old to be a farmer, maybe, or a father—but hers.

When Suzanne's plane (her friend Robert's, actually, who was the pilot, herself Rob's guest, his passenger) hit, in midair, the other small private plane also flying low over the Tanana at midnight (the Tanana a river, a tributary of the Yukon that glides light brown as mud but coated then like magic with sunlight, flowing,

30

flowing, slowly but so swift through the heart of Alaska in summer, in July, the night light like midday but actually midnight; too high up, there, for mosquitoes even—high, high, above the river of light) Suzanne says that she thought—hitting—only of her parents.

This will hurt them so much, she thought. My dying will hurt them so much.

And—

And—who would believe that dying could happen so slowly? Slow, slow and soft as the fall from heaven of feathers. This too was a thought, a dying thought, says Suzanne.

Not that it should be fast, no—but slow, slow, so slow, more slow than a slow dance of love.

But Suzanne did not die (nor Leslie, rolling alone in her station wagon—slow, slow, slow too) nor the pilot Rob nor the three other persons in the other small plane, but all only sank slowly together into the Tanana.

Yes, they all sank together into that light, into some bright silty sink of salvation, swirling like magic—gliding—floating—waltzing in silted sun, there in some earthy heaven where the two planes flirted and swooned together till the rescue came, by outboard motor. And the planes were like boats, too: toy boats in a vast glittery bathtub.

I can't die, Leslie thought in her station wagon, rolling alone.

I can't die because I have too much work to do—not her painting only or the cooking, the wash, the bathing, cleaning, bill-paying, hand-squeezing, back-

31

rubbing, scolding, hugging, chewing-sitting-standing-walking-talking-sleeping-waking and comfort of flesh and bone only, but the larger work of love.

A slow work, too, of the mind and heart, like snow.

White, white, the tile and the walls and the bed.

Leslie stands at the hospital window watching the snow: snowflakes still blizzarding down on Fairbanks, in March, when last week it might have been, with the sun—except for the mounded and crusted snow everywhere—spring.

It might have been spring, but with Libby Riddles still on the trail and Susan Butcher still singing, somewhere, to her dogs; it might; but today the snowflakes are traveling for her, traveling and traveling backward for Leslie into the heart of winter.

This headache is a way of loving, too, a way of rolling and rolling into a past that is also the future, and touching again all the people she has always and already loved.

The world is a tunnel, too, into which she rolls to find and lose the people she loves, as in a blizzard—one foot of visibility ahead only—whiteout, whiteout—

And she does not love them well enough—except that they know she tries, and they too try, and our fat little fox terriers hop and hop around us—the miner's dogs as he lifts the turkeys (fat dogs, not even bird-sized, though it is Mom's night vision this time: how a man in her dream offered her $200 for Toy or maybe Jerry, not for Lollie, and she of course said no; no price high enough for this fine dog—)

Into the Heart of Winter

Hopping, hopping everywhere—yapping and nip-
ping, flipping in somersaults on the hard-packed dirt
floor of the hovel that is the cabin and that leads like
a secret into the hand-dug mine—
The mine that tunnels deep—deep, deep into the
heart of winter.

And she'll help bake six turkeys for the miner's one
old bald-headed brother Sam—(Skinny Sam, a man so
old and wrinkled now, far too small for his skin—)
while the four fox terriers leap and fall and hop around
us, yapping like Christmas. (Four: all fat, all gray-
haired, a mother and three elderly dog siblings—)

And we bend and bend toward the woodstove again
and again, lifting six steaming heavy savory beautiful
turkeys from the oven for his brother—and Leslie's
parents have come feasting, too, from the train station
in Fairbanks, and Suzanne's also through the air, as a
miracle, following Sam—all, all—traveling here into the
heart of winter, journeying through this blizzard and
the heat and steam of fresh-baked turkeys and the bal-
let of yapping dogs, to give and accept this whiteout
miracle we call love.

Vreelund

He wore *lederhosen*. Like a child, Amanda thought, rubbing at her eyes, or a circus performer.

The slide was projected onto a sheet tacked to the log wall of the cabin, so that Vreelund's short, stocky form rayed out from the hillside in ripples, his bare knees shimmering wetly and his chest pocked and ridged, like the surface of a pond touched by soft wind. Maybe there was a draft someplace? Amanda peered through the brilliant shaft of light from the projector to find its source, but could not.

Church was talking. "This one's taken on the West Buttress, above the Kahiltna Glacier." Church bent into the cave of light made by the projector and pointed, his voice reverent, awed. He wrinkled his nose and squinted too, pushing up at the nosepiece of his glasses with his thumb and forefinger in a quick gesture of self-doubt that Amanda, who'd met him for the first time tonight, already recognized as definitive.

Church was a tall, bearded, ascetic-looking person dressed in army fatigues and wornout jogging shoes, and the slides showing "The Wildman John Vreelund and His Mountain Exploits," as the flier at the library had proclaimed, belonged to him. Church seemed to Amanda someone so unalterably opposed to authority, on principle, that this opposition ruled him like a des-

35

pot; his reverential voice and the slightly uncomfortable proprietary air would both be explicable from that perspective. Poor Church was probably just trying to set the tone of the occasion, Amanda told herself, and the tone was to be worshipful, as befitting a memorial service for the late, great, wondrous and so oddly misremembered John Vreelund. But how does one relate to a living legend? Or a dead one? It was her own problem too.

"Christ, Rob," called a voice from the corner of the room. Kreuger, Amanda decided; it was Kreuger, Vreelund's climbing partner in an early venture. Kreuger was a raspy-voiced, aggressive, orange-haired man whom she'd met months ago. "We all *know* where the West Buttress is. Half of us have *climbed* McKinley." *Denali*, Amanda thought. ("*Call her Denali, Mandy—*") Like Vreelund, she preferred the Indian name: *the great one*. "Get on to Mt. Huntington and Moose Tooth," Kreuger said. "We want time to break into committees."

"Committees, Frank, God—" came a husky, almost teary female voice in the darkness. Amanda could attach no name to the voice. "Kreuger would break the Second Coming into committees."

Other stirrings and sighs, softly-voiced words, bits of dry laughter moved through the crowd. People were standing or squatting everywhere, angled into doorways, leaning against walls, and sitting on the seats and arms of the room's few pieces of battered furniture. One middle-aged woman held her body in what looked to Amanda like a yoga posture on the center of the coffee table; her eyes were closed. Like Amanda, the others sat elbow-to-elbow—"arse to arse," Vree-

36

lund would have said—on the floor of the darkened main room of the cabin.

The cabin belonged to Church too, and woodsmoke was the dominant smell, then sweat, Amanda decided, and something like mold—odd in the dry air of Fairbanks—or wet leather. Though there was pot too, marijuana, its Spanish name so beautiful—

But perhaps the common choice of the word pot—or grass, weed—signified some allegiance to clarity, some attempt to see use of the mind-fuzzying *cannabis* coolly, in a less-than-sentimental light? Amanda, whose own tenderness (or sentimentality?) was a constant burden to her, liked that interpretation. Yet perhaps it was only a thought borne on the draughts of inhaled smoke—? She sighed aloud.

Church was talking again, another slide.

And Amanda, who'd come here sacrilegiously probably, a disbeliever at this meeting organized to find a suitably sanctifying memorial for John Vreelund, coughed. Forbearance. She mouthed the word silently, trying not to move her lips. It seemed impossible to watch any more of this deification process. Instead she rested her forehead against her knees, moving carefully to avoid body contact with her nearest floormates. Once in position, she could smell again the true grass scent that lingered on her denim jeans.

She was a big woman, shy and serious looking, a special ed teacher, and she wore jeans almost always now. The down-and-out clothing style of Church and some of the others here seemed to her affected—too pointedly shabby, or mock-woodsy and false. But her jeans were not an affectation at all. They were a practical choice, almost an occupational uniform. Work with the seven trainable kids in this year's primary—

all of whom drooled—made jeans a necessity. Besides, on principles as firm, she supposed, as any silly conviction held by Church, she detested all things phony or contrived or calculated. The quality she loved most in retarded children, in fact, was their simple honesty, their complete freedom from guile.

But perhaps that bias—for surely such a stance constituted a bias, a quirk—might explain her feelings for Vreelund? She thought it suddenly. He had been so— so genuinely and honestly bizarre. It was sheer chance that someone like herself had known him at all, sheer chance that she'd rented the other half of the rundown duplex he'd lived in until his—his disappearance—? His death—? His final ascent and transfiguration—? What should it be called when the body had never been found? She coughed again.

Of course, she'd had four months to ponder all this too, for she'd given up on him in June. If he had not returned to Fairbanks for Solstice, she reasoned, he must be— Whatever. Dead was only a word she made herself say in company, now that October had arrived. Dead, dead, dead, like the body of his cat Dixie, whose bloody carcass had, somehow, begun everything.

Amanda glanced at the current slide: an ice peak shimmering in the sun, with Vreelund showing as a small oddly motion-filled form who looked back over one rippling shoulder. To wave at the camera—? His right arm was extended but still, bent slightly at the thick wrist. "Mt. Huntington," said Church reverently. "July 1980."

Amanda thought she had loved him too—if it was possible to love the infuriating John Vreelund. And it was not the "love" that usually proved to be infatuation—not sex or lust, for she'd felt all that often enough.

Not an ordinary passion at all, really, and nothing akin to Church's starry-eyed deification, but a kind of overwhelming affinity, perhaps? The gentle compassion of one hopeless loser for another—? (*"Bizarre, Ms. Amanda—"*)

But things *had* started off "horror-show," as John had liked to say, for she'd run over Dixie in the driveway, the mangy cat she'd been feeding for a week on her back porch, unaware that it belonged to her odd-looking neighbor. Yet all that was something she wanted to forget—an incredible accident.

It was better to remember how she and John had eaten together sometimes, Vreelund making his special stir-fries in the cast iron skillet that he'd said he used for *"everything but coffee and oatmeal."* And she washing carrots, or slicing tomatoes or apples or Tillamook cheese, sometimes a loaf of sourdough bread when one or the other of them had found time to bake or remembered to stop at Foodland.

And he sang while he cooked. Did the others here know that? It was "Swanee" this time, the time she was remembering; for suddenly it *was* a specific memory rather than the general blur of odd little suppers it had been at first:

"How I luv-ya, how I luv-ya, my dear old Swaneee—"

She was spooning rice onto the yellowed Melmac plates. She could smell it all too, the grimy fried-grease scent of his kitchen, then the stir-fry of canned shrimp, of green onions and red cabbage and broccoli Vreelund grew in the tiny backyard of the duplex on 9th Avenue, then kept cool in his *"half-dead, mungy freezer."* The freezer was a relic of a downtown fire, its enamel surface blackened to a stark flatness, a total absence of color that made the substantial, boxy, upright thing an oddly ghostlike form in the corner of his kitchen, except for the shiny spot near the top of the door—like a halo—where the white enamel had crazed and shimmered faintly through the soot.

"I'd give the world to be—"

And mimeographed sheets that were to be his campaign fliers were everywhere—on the countertop and table and both seats of the two battered chairs, for it was early October too, in the memory—almost exactly one year ago.

"Among the folks in—"

And they'd met a week or so earlier, with her killing of the cat— John's face a horrid mask then, yelling curses at her through the missing glass of his storm door, his thick little form stomping down the steps toward her, all this just after the time he'd signed up to run for the School Board—

"D-I-X-I-E-ven know—"

It was a ludicrous idea, of course. *"John Vreelund, the zonked-out hippie freak,"* as he loved to call himself, running against *"six or seven straight guys,"* as he always called *them*, Amanda dutifully reminding him that four of the other candidates were females, that they all ran by seats besides, so his opponent was actually "only *one* straight female." She'd even phrased it all in his terms.

But the truth was that he seldom used the "zonked-out hippie" description in his absurd campaign anyway. "JOHN VREELUND LOVES YOUR KIDS." That was his formal campaign slogan. (*"Let 'em sweat that one, Mandy,"* he'd say, leering evilly.)

He was running on a platform of drugs and free sex for kids, and he'd appeared twice on radio—once on a call-in show where a listener screamed at him over the phone that he was "possessed by Satan." John loved to repeat that charge for her, his voice taking on a country drawl, his eyes glazing while he assured her that the emphasis *had* to be placed on the first syllable: "*PO-ssessed. It's necessary, Mandy*," he'd say, pronouncing it again and again: "*PO-ssessed—*"

There had been two or three TV appearances too, one a debate during which John had taken off one shoe (a rubber thong, actually) and thumped it again and again on the narrow wooden conference table. ("*Like Kruschev*," he'd said. "*Remember the filmclips?*") He'd also flapped his head backward and forward many times, so that his long, hemp-colored, kinky hair sloshed around his head like frothy water.

But they'd talked for the first time because of another TV interview—the events following the death of the cat being ones she blocked from her mind, and not "talk" at all but insane shouting (his) and ridiculous tears (hers), with nothing worth considering there except that first glimpse of her neighbor's possible madness, his certain genius for profanity, and her own typical loser's behavior, compounded by luckless circumstance.

Their first real talk had come two or three days later, during the final taped TV interview, with Amanda fixing Campbell's chunky soup for her supper at the stove in her kitchen and watching through the doorway "the wildman candidate" being questioned on her TV screen in the living room, while, through the kitchen window, she suddenly glimpsed the same small kinky-haired figure—the cat's owner, for God's sake!—

crouched in the backyard pulling up the last of his carrots through a thin, crusted layer of snow.

She'd thought again that he was insane. But something—like a dare to herself perhaps, or that persistent desire to cast aside sentimentality—had made her switch off the set and call to him from the window: "Hello. Ah, well—I mean, excuse me, but aren't you—Vreelund?"

"*Ah, fame*—" he'd said, rising and turning toward her so quickly that she'd entirely forgotten the fear that had caught in her throat just after the words escaped from her mouth. What might a madman—or a "wildman"—do?

He had, in fact, lunged up to the window with a bunch of dirt-encrusted carrots drooping from his right hand: "*A bouquet for the lady. Peace offering*—?"

She'd been tempted to close the window on his wrist, but his face had supported such a huge, expansive grin that she reached out and shook the carrots sedately instead, like an offered hand.

"*Vreelund, ma'am,*" he'd said, clicking the heels of his thongs. "*Candidate at your service.*" She'd decided then that there must be something to this Vreelund beyond insanity.

And her determination not to be sentimental had overcome her again. She'd accepted the carrots, then said what she was thinking: "How can you do it? I mean, how can you make a fool of yourself like that before the whole town?"

His grin had disappeared, his light-green eyes shifting and glinting (with what? anger? humor? actual madness—?) before the wonderful grin began again. And she'd felt it for the first time then, with the grin's return—that absolute affinity.

42

"Sheer courage, ma'am," he'd said. *"Guts, et cetera. Complete and total wrong-headed bravery."* Then he'd bowed formally, from the waist, and Amanda had known that she would love this strange John Vreelund.

But perhaps all this was sentimentality too? Like her choice of jobs—a charge Mother had made once, in a quarrel. But if teaching retarded kids had originally been a sentimental choice, surely now, after five years, that fluffy-headed emotion was banished—? As knowledge of *"the real downhome Vreelund,"* as he'd called himself to her once, had banished sentimentality about him—? But she could not be sure, and she coughed a third time, opening her eyes to stare briefly at John's squat form´ bent over a coil of rope, the seat of his *lederhosen* shimmering beside a blue glacier.

Would any of them—or she—idealize him so if he'd lived? Even if the climb had been successful? Was his death proving to be not the Great Equalizer at all but the great sentimentality mill? He'd so often seemed ridiculous, alive. Were they all simple-minded chumps? *Cheechakos* at love and life and the bestowing of honor, taken in by this odd little pitchman of a climber?

This was only the start of her second year of teaching in Fairbanks; she'd lived in Alaska for six weeks when she'd met John. But she'd wintered here now, and so was, at least technically, no longer a true *cheechako*, no longer a tenderfoot, a "Chicago," as the Athabaskans had begun to call newcomers years and years ago, the corrupted and misshapen word sticking. They themselves, the Athabaskan Indians, were *Dena* or *Tena* in all dialects—*the people.*

Amanda liked that. Maybe life in Alaska would make others deserve the name "people" too? Like the Yiddish *mensch*—? And her lashes brushed denim luxuriantly while Church's voice droned.

She had been born and raised in Chicago, though; that much in the Indian epithet was correct. Like Vreelund. But he'd run away from home when he was twelve—"*a bizarre fact in the great man's life, Amanda*—"

And the suppers *had* surely been bizarre—like their meeting, like his response to her unintentional killing of the cat, like everything about Vreelund. Yet fun and exciting too, memorable, so that she was lifting one of the mimeographed sheets now, fingering it carefully again in her memory, smelling the damp, inky, alcohol smell, then putting aside the wooden spoon she'd been using to dish up rice and reading aloud:

"LOOK YOURSELF IN THE MIRROR'S EYE AGAIN: VOTE VREELUND! It's ridiculous, John. Completely absurd. Madness! This 'mirror's eye' business, for instance. And this one: THE PEOPLE'S CHOICE—VREELUND—RUNNING BY POPULAR DEMAND. Nobody asked you to run—"

"*A technicality, Mandy. A technicality*—"

"And you're certainly no—Everyman. Not by a long shot!" He'd stopped stirring and grabbed a pencil to jot that one on the back of a smudged sheet: VREELUND—FAIRBANKS' EVERYMAN—WINNER BY A LONG SHOT!! But she'd ignored him.

"How many votes can you hope to get? And it's cost you—what? Three-hundred dollars so far?" She knew she was nagging, butting in, mothering—but he was such a child.

"*One-hundred-thirteen dollars and twenty-six cents. It's a bargain, Mandy. Best fun I've had. And a tax shelter! All deductible, every penny*—"

"If you had an income—" For she already knew by then that he lived on food stamps and infrequent checks from his maternal grandmother in Chicago, plus the occasional sale of homegrown marijuana. His rent was months overdue— And she was feeling suddenly like his parent, one's first and most enduring loyal opponent: Time for homework, Johnny, and when *will* you comb your hair—? But in this case her loyalty was to something usually called sanity—

He'd lifted the skillet from the propane stove then. From her superior height, the flame from the burner glowed behind him like a perfect halo of blue and yellow light, she moving to turn the knob to OFF while he spooned the stir-fry onto the rice. She was smelling ginger now, his favorite spice. And then he'd said it, the words that might be the point of this memory. (*"If things have to HAVE a point, Amanda. But why, dammit?"*)

"See, it isn't who you are or what you do that counts in life. See, Mandy, SEE—? It's the intensity of your dance. I believe in the life dance. The intensity of the life dance—"

And a shiver of something—like horror or fear—had run down her spine.

She could remember no more of the evening, though she tried now, covering her ears with her hands for a moment to shut out Church's voice—until her right elbow brushed the biceps of someone beside her, who squirmed and cleared his throat.

Okay. She'd reconstruct each scene without motion—a still life, her own slide show, with no sentimentality:

Vreelund

John, screaming obscenities in the driveway, the cat suspended by its tail from his hand.

John, at the stove, bent forward, humming, stirring veggies into his skillet with the long metal fork he always used for cooking.

John, turning to grin at her: a short, sturdy, thick-haired man—shaggy, bearded, five-foot-two or three, his face childishly handsome, and his kinky hair pulled back and fastened with a red rubberband.

John, wearing cutoff jeans and a t-shirt that said COORS BEER, singing "Swanee" and tap dancing, barefoot, to his own tune. (*"Buck'n'wing, Mandy—"*)

John, a man barely twenty-four, at most twenty-six (for she was not even certain of his age—!) wearing swim trunks, a sweatshirt, and mountaineer boots, and standing with one foot resting on the seat of a kitchen chair (her kitchen chair this time, and a decent chair: Thanksgiving Day); John, waving his left arm while he read to her from his poem, his book-length poem, his damned silly obsession of an epic poem that surely caught madness on its hook like a silvery fish—

Then herself, poised over his kitchen table like a pink-faced monolith, chopping onions for the stir-fry.

Tall: *"Six-three!"* John had said once, shortly after TV's introduction and his gift of carrots. He'd leered up at her from the front yard—that next afternoon, possibly?—while she climbed the steps to her own side of the duplex. *"Wow! Six-THREE. Eat much—?"* And in that way, he'd invited her for the first time to share his supper.

Herself, slightly heavy, though she did not *"eat much."* 186 pounds, actually. A surprisingly gangly woman, given her weight. And Jewish-looking. ("But

46

I *am* Jewish, Mother—like you. So how should I look?"
That had always been her response to her mother's
vague complaint, to Mother's perpetual sad-eyed litany, that widow's lament of a charge, that she'd never
"manage to find a husband," because she looked "*so*
Jewish.")

Yes, she could see it all: herself, Amanda, that South-
ern mammy's name like a nondenominational cross
to bear—the class wit in fifth grade, making it "Aunt
Jemanda," which had stuck for years. Amanda, the
name given by her dead father, who'd died of leukemia
three weeks before her birth and apparently chosen
the name in some final burst of Northern white liberal
fervor. *Amanda*—"worthy to be loved," in *Webster's
Collegiate Dictionary*—a joke!

Herself: straight-cut schoolgirl's long hair dangling
in limp black finger curls over the lumpy shoulders—
because her hair, uncombed for an hour, always fell
into finger curls, and damned if she'd betray her natural self (whatever *that* was) by having it straightened
or shorn; wide face serious, as befitting the full con-
centration required of one engaged in the task of chopping green onions; her plastic horn-rim glasses sliding
down her nose just as Church's did; her shoulders
slumping a bit with that droop that Mother had warned
against (a second motherly litany) for more years than
Jewishness—

Herself, with a pouchy belly at twenty-nine, though
she'd never even felt it filled with child; only twice
with semen, for that matter—

And how odd that there was no sensation to that,
no heat, no fullness—for she'd come to Alaska not
only to escape Mother but to nurse what had then
seemed a broken heart—

47

Twenty-nine *then*, of course. Thirty now. Over the hill. Belly still childless and still pouchy—

An "old maid" indeed? Though no longer a "maiden," of course—

Not even "in love" with this insane "wildman" she seemed to love. This madman who was, perhaps—even dead—more like the little brother she'd never had—or the child? The forbidden, strange friend—? More like a catalyst in her life—yes, that!—than a lover.

But a catalyst for what?

And she could hear the rest of the conversation now, because they *had* had it after all:

"Dance— Life dance—! Ah—stop, John!" But she'd felt it again then, the chill running along her spine as he'd glanced up at her with that quick, betrayed look. The same chill she'd felt in the driveway while she'd freed the cat's body from the front wheels of the Subaru and heard the yelling begin. Yet she'd gone on:

"Because there *is* such a thing as maturity, John. As common sense. There is such a thing as restraint and—and loyalty to one's own species. Oh, shoot! I sound like my mother. But it's *real*, John— making one want to use one's energy to do something—something enduring. Something significant and—and *serious*."

"*You malign me, ma'am*," he'd said, bending to spoon out his stir-fry, then turning toward her again, suddenly, his face oddly sad for a second. "*And I am serious, Mandy. I'm serious. I'm nothing if not serious.*" Then he'd soft-shoed across the torn linoleum, grinning absurdly again, swinging the empty cast iron skillet like an Eskimo drum.

But two months later, after the election where he'd garnered five votes, not one of them Mandy's, he'd announced the climb.

It was to be *"a serious venture, Ms. Amanda,"* a winter climb up the North Peak. This was the side of McKinley closest to Fairbanks, though John had always called the mountain Denali too, of course— (*"Call her Denali, Mandy. She's a she, you know—"*)

And maybe he was right? A female noun, from *Dena*—? The name for a single human as well as the group, and the *-li* ending possibly denoting feminine gender rather than just vastness or huge size? Or both perhaps—? Named by a matrilineal people, after all—

But she'd have to study, to research all this carefully, before it was even fair to speculate—

He'd climbed Denali before, of course. Both the North and South Peaks, but that had been in summer, and with others. This time the climb would begin in late January, and he'd be alone. That would be a new record.

"Something serious, AND significant, Mandy—"

"Oh, Cripes, John. You're hopeless!"

And she might have felt guilty about her own hand in this new and ridiculous venture—this ultimately deadly venture—except that it was so obviously a Vreelund project. So obviously part of the natural progression in a life which had grown ever more— What? Just "bizarre," as John himself suggested? Wild? Laughable? Self-destructive? Arrhythmic? Or simply inexplicable—?

"This isn't a joke, John," she'd said. "Life isn't a joke. People do not make jokes with their own flesh and blood. Why not March? Or May?"

"*M again*," he'd answered. "*M—M—M—. Boring, boring, boring. You have got to watch out for that tendency in yourself, Amanda. You tend to go in a bit too heavily for boredom.*"

But the real reasons for the climb were two, which she soon knew by heart. He *was* "a serious climber" after all—had climbed each of the most common routes on Denali at least once, not to mention Hunter and Foraker and Mt. St. Elias. While he was in his teens, he'd been a member of the second party ever to climb the Kachatna Spire, the highest of the Cathedral Spires. And in the late seventies he'd climbed the Revelation Mountains, a remote group in the southwestern part of the Alaska Range—mountains so remote, John said, that they were not visible from any inhabited land. ("*Eternal, Mandy. That's what I think of as eternal—being there.*")

He was "serious." He'd even written intelligibly about his climbs for a respected mountaineering journal. Intelligently, even. Sensitively. Rather humbly and with poetic beauty, some of his passages attaching themselves permanently to one's mind—

He'd written about the climbs of others too, and he loved to tell the tale of the group of inexperienced Fairbanks residents, not one of them a trained climber, who'd been first to scale Denali in 1910. They'd set out in mid-winter too, "*financed by some bored businessmen and saloonkeeps.*" They'd reached the North Peak in March, making the last 8500 feet of the climb in a single day. Then they'd erected a huge U.S. flag that they hoped could be seen from Fairbanks, sighted through a telescope. (*"It could, Mandy. Of course it could!"*)

She'd read about that climb after hearing his version, in a climbers' handbook that called it, "one of the most astonishing ventures in the history of mountaineering." Well, John's venture was to be even more "astonishing."

And that, of course, was his second and most important reason for the climb, she'd decided. Not simple exhibitionism, but the desire to create astonishment. That "intensity of the life dance" of his—

And in that way, she thought now, feeling her throat muscles constrict just as they had when TV news in Fairbanks had finally and officially declared him "dead"—yes, in that way John *was* perhaps most truly Alaskan, most truly an Everyman here—and yet most markedly set apart and separate and eccentric. In his whole-hearted love of "astonishment." In his wild-eyed willingness to create the outsized heroic gesture—

But the climb was more than a gesture. He'd carry his own special "meal," a lightweight powdery white mixture of bleached flour, powdered sugar, powdered milk, and powdered eggs. (*"Light, economical, nutritious, quickly digested, and my own private recipe—"*) She'd helped him package it in plastic lunch bags— each, he said, holding just the right amount for a single meal. (*"Great cooked or raw, Mandy—"*)

It had taken four evenings to package enough of the mixture for the trip, the two of them working in his drafty kitchen through four ice-foggy mid-January nights, while she taught days and he spent the sunlit

51

hours walking across town to assemble supplies and beg a few donations.

"They look like bags of cocaine, John. Or, anyway, the way I imagine bags of cocaine would look."

John nodding: *"Ah, hah! Once again you've uncovered one of my secret diversions, Ms. Amanda. Fun on the mountain. I call it Russian roulette with coke. Will this be a baggy of true nutrition or a snort of sudden inspiration? A new high atop the sweet Big One— I can only afford one bag of coke, of course, so the odds are against me. Or for me, depending on point of view—"*

"Oh, God, John. Don't joke that way. It's dangerous enough in winter without— Oh, you wouldn't, would you? You wouldn't—?" She'd leaned across the table ready to pound playfully on his shoulders with both fists, when it occurred to her suddenly that this was something they'd never done— Touch.

And she'd felt the cold shiver along her spine again.

But his third reason for the climb, as Mandy saw it, was more complex. Both subconscious and sexual— and far more deeply mad than the other reasons. It had come to her while he was reading his poem aloud, two nights before he left. His epic poem. The poem that had run to two forty-page stanzas at the time she'd met him—eighty or ninety handwritten pages, all dedicated to "Her"—to Denali:

> you
> swirl your gauzy scarves
> away then round
> you and I burn, my heart swelling
> its desire into a cry
> that sears my lips

a howl
the call of snow-bleached
wolves

It was a love poem—"*your breath wakes / me,
shakes the tent / we writhe together*"—an epic love
poem to the mountain. John could begin at any point,
reading a few lines, penciling in revisions as he read,
and he was "*gone*"—enthralled, entranced—"*gone—*"
("*She's freaked me again, Mandy— My Lady—*")
He called the poem only "She," and Amanda, when
she first heard him read from it (in her kitchen on
Thanksgiving Day, while the turkey sizzled and wafted
its savory smells from the oven) was at once full of
that shivery cold of a shudder again. Chilled. Then,
suddenly, jealous—yes, that!—then shocked. And finally frightened, that shivery feeling invading her body
again—
Madness? A dementia produced by drugs? Or the
final budding in John of some long-incipient schizo-
phrenia? Though he was harmless, surely— Harmless—

He'd given the manuscript to her, the day before
he'd started his climb—January 23. ("*Guard it with
your life, Amanda—*") But she could not touch it. It
still lay on an unused shelf in her kitchen, absorbing
the noise from the young family that now occupied
Vreelund's side of the duplex. Certainly she could not
yet look at the poem. Just as she could not look at
Denali, white and ghostly, on the rare days when "she"
was visible, gleaming like a vast Spirit, a pale and luminous pyramid of stone and ice seen from more than
one-hundred-fifty miles—
She could not look without feeling tears sting her
eyes or that constriction in her throat—and now, since

September, a sense of herself changed forever by all
this, transfigured in a way that did not show in any
mirror.

There was a kind of genius to the poem, of course—
a vastness and richness and originality that she could
only think of as that—"genius."

But it was absurd too. Mad. Written in scrawls and
swiggles on dirty, wrinkled notebook paper and the
flattened back of grocery sacks, with arrows and
blotches indicating deletions and additions, changes
that never quite became anything like a "completed
text."

Living the poem seemed, for John, the thing. His
life dance, maybe—

But now she was leaning back against the knees behind her. Feeling sick, feeling faint; knowing, finally,
that John was dead and would never again recite his
absurd poem for her. Would never again soft-shoe in
his kitchen, or sing, making his stir-fry—

And she should be howling or crying or laughing
wildly somewhere. Anywhere. It was the least she could
do. Because John's "life dance" had been real, whatever it meant, and it was finished now—

But of course no one here—herself included—had
really known John at all, and the memorial that they
(we, yes, *we*!) would try to offer would be only a mon-
ument to ourselves, to this deadly "sanity" the rest of
us called life—

Yet none of this was tragedy or heroism, dammit.
No message here at all, just a force of life as real and
mysterious as Denali—

54

And maybe that noise was herself? A soft howling—
A moaning—

> and I burn, my heart swelling
> its desire into a cry
> that sears my lips
>
> a howl

Skin

On the sidewalk outside Co-Op Drug, and in the street, drunks shimmered like mirages. Lucy watched them from Co-Op's entryway, their slow steps twisted by the door glass to a dance that swayed and wavered, ugly, catching the noon heat. The sight made her think, miserably, of her girlhood, these Second Avenue drunks in Fairbanks so like all the ones she remembered from home, from Rampart, drunken Indians. One of those Rampart drunks had been her youngest uncle, and she could still—even after the sliding away of forty-five years—not think of Uncle Ralph without seeing saliva— Or a thick string of drool, maybe— Saliva, which hung always, it seemed in her memory, from Uncle Ralph's lips—

He'd died of drink. At twenty-seven. There at home, dragged in from the riverbank to die quietly in her parents' bed, not of TB as they said in Rampart, but of drink. She'd been eleven, her face hidden (for days after, it seemed—) for days (and before—) in the dusty, warm peace of the dog's coat, there on the porch. The old dog, Scout he had been, panting, panting, so warm. And her whole face and body pressed down on the porch floor into deepest dog—

Now she opened one glass door slowly and stepped out, dry heat rising from the cement like old wind.

She stopped there where she stood, her white slacks glowing as cloud above the yellow plastic luster of her sandals. And the door's swish and thud behind her was a sound erasing all her careful intent—which had been to stride, purposefully, through these clusters of wavering, shabby men (and some women, too) who were "visiting"— "Visiting" here on the sidewalk in Fairbanks— Drunks. To walk among these drunks without looking to left or to right, until she reached the parking lot and the cool, dark safety of the Lincoln—

Instead she stood still, her heart thumping as she pulled sunglasses from the flowery pouch that was the front of her *kuspuk* blouse and adjusted the silvery ear hooks. With two fingers (fingers which shook stupidly) she pushed against the nosepiece, its sheen of glass stars rough to her fingertips even when she was sure the glasses rode squarely upon the short bridge of her nose, and—yes, all the world was green. She straightened her spine then and stepped forward again, the hot air surging, catching up her face and her body in thickened heat as she left the pale shade of Co-Op's marquee—

Maybe Howard had been right. He had not wanted her to come. She had, Howard said, her reputation to consider. "Watch and see, Lucy," he'd said. "You'll be sorry. You'll dirty those new sandals in sidewalk beer. Or vomit—" And he'd frowned with the face of his own joke, those last words of Howard's still following her when she backed the perfect, ten-year-old Lincoln down the driveway at eleven. Its air conditioner beginning to hum and her eyes seeing only the dishes stacked neatly in the dish drainer, Howard's pipe in

Skin

his one hand and the striped dish towel draped over his shoulder in just that way she always told him not—

And she'd driven downtown so slowly, careful, those words humming: "You'll be sorry—" And herself walking so slowly then, half dazed, and trying, trying to feel—casual. Walking at first (like practice) through Penney's bright aisles, dazed— Because in Penney's you never saw drunks.

But Co-Op was doing July inventory, had advertised rabbit skins. White and cross rabbits too, as it turned out. More fine than the newspaper sketch she had smoothed with her fingers on the kitchen table, for Howard. Two thick and beautiful stacks of them, so soft and silky and luxurious, though of course only rabbits— For 79¢ each. It was a bargain. She could not remember seeing such a bargain. And Roxanne, her own only grandchild, and Rita's only daughter, was pregnant for the first time. Only—? As Rita was Lucy's (and Howard's) own only daughter, only—? Their only child— For Howard had not been— And she herself, no—

But surely Roxanne would produce a female child. Another beauty. The fourth, in generations, she would be— And these rabbit skins would become a new baby bunting for her. Booties too, yes— Beautiful and white, with those soft, soft red-brown spots like patches of time caught up— And— Beautiful.

Lucy pulled the crackly pinkness of the plastic Co-Op sack (filled up with the sixteen cross-rabbit skins) tight against her breasts and began to step off the curb. Second Avenue was a smell like beer and sweat, the hot breath of cars— And noise that swelled in your ears— But those rabbit skins had all been gentle and

59

clean, pure to your fingers, there in Co-Op, and she would begin the bunting today. This afternoon—

Because skin sewing was something you could love safely. An Indian thing, for she remembered her aunts and her grandma and sometimes even Mama, too, sewing skins, in Rampart. And Howard could tease her about it, though he rarely did anymore. Because people were beginning to call her "an Athabaskan artist" now. A skin sewer. "Preserving a traditional art form." That was what that last woman, from the Arts Association, had said. In the school, in May—

But once, that one time only, Howard calling her "my skinny squaw"— That time when Roxanne (a little girl then) had braided the long neckcurls— (Herself Roxanne's own "Mem-mem" then—) Roxanne braiding Mem-mem's "little Orphan Annie perm," which was what Howard still always called this hairstyle— (Because he'd chosen it: "One of the first ones in Fairbanks too, Lucy!" His face proud, beaming—) Those neckcurls twisted into a single short cluster of braid: "My skinny squaw—"

But Howard had always been more a father. Twelve years older— She, always, "the baby," the prettiest and youngest, at home too, back in Rampart. And—

And it was no lie to live now in their own suburban house. A clean and beautiful home. Her neatly-boxed skins all kept in the pantry beside the dishwasher. No lie to love— Because, yes, she did love the skins— Sewing them. Touching—

And Howard was an Indian too, of course.

And she felt only sometimes that small twinge of something (like shame it seemed, though that was ridiculous—) when she and Howard went (as they so

often did now) to address the grade school children in
Fairbanks. Telling those children— Telling them, now
that Howard had sold his optical shop and retired completely— (Two years ago that was—) Telling all those
sweet gardens of child faces what it was to be an Indian— (The soles of the yellow sandals sticking— In
beer, maybe—? Not—? But almost across now, to the
parking lot, yes, there soon—)

And, yes, you could love skin sewing—

"The skins were always clean, that's what I remember," she'd said last May, her mind—and her soul too—
pulling away from her so strangely there as she stood
on that cool, foreign little stage— (For the stages, in
the gyms they were always, never really became—)
There, during the most recent grade school visit. In
May, it was— And Howard staring so strangely across
the stage into her face, shaking his head slightly,
frowning that small, small frown—

"The skins were always clean—" Her own voice.
"The fur was warmer that way, warm and clean. And
the Indian people, back home, the old people, they
shook them carefully. Before and after using them,
they shook them to keep them clean. And there was
a fine, pure scent too—" Shaking her own head— "I
don't know— They cared for them, though, it's true.
Hung them from moose or caribou horns on the walls
of the cabins inside, yes, sometimes. And they were
beautiful. So beautiful— Some made into parkas and
hats and the small baby things— Or blankets crocheted
from strips of rabbit skin— So soft and always clean—
Always—" Howard's small frown—

Oh, it frightened you, to feel your own mind dance
away from you like that, carrying something—your
soul or your spirit— Carrying your whole self dancing

away into some past that seemed almost a future, and seemed right— Yes, right.

And now someone was saying, a voice behind her saying: "Lucy. Goddamn, Lucy, that's you—"

And she was turning to meet the voice. And yes, yes— No.

It was George. For thirty-five years, maybe, she had not seen him once. George. And he still stood like a skinny boy there, slim and wiry as any boy—but balder, a little— His body wavering before her eyes. George.

And he was hugging her then and the rabbit skins, hugging— That plastic sack crackling between them there, in the street in front of— While cars moved around them and someone laughed—

"Oh, George," she said, her own voice saying it. "George— George—"

"Goddamn if it isn't you," he said. "Goddamn if it isn't you, Lucy." No drool from his lips and he smelled only of cigarettes, but his body still— Yes. It wavered away from her and then close again— And tears, yes, tears. She was weeping against his chest. Cigarette smoke—

"Don't cry, Lucy," George said. "Come have a beer." And he was holding the sack, the pink crackly sack of rabbit skins under his right arm, pushed way up under his armpit, her shoulders held tight with his left arm— Weeping, she— He taking the sunglasses from her face and leading her across the street and in— Yes— Into the worst bar of them all. The worst Native bar where Lucy had never, ever been before—

"You look—" she said, trying not to cry—

"Firefighting," George said. "I've been firefighting. At Nenana—" And he was grinning, hugging her again, his body smoky but with cigarettes only— And she— yes, crying, hugging—

"Thirty-five years," George said. "Thirty-five. Yes, Lucy, it's you." And he was hugging her again.

"Two beers," George said. "Two," holding up two fingers toward the back of— And people were looking— A laugh— And a chair, yes, a chair— George was fitting her body to that dirty-looking kitchen chair.

"A beer," George said, pushing the glass into her fingers. "You look fine," he said, "not like an old lady, Lucy—"

"And you—" Only crying a little— "George. Oh, George—"

"Well, we should have," he said, putting his own glass on the table with both hands. "When we were eighteen in Rampart, Lucy, we should have got married and be damned if—"

And her whole life— No, no. He could not take her whole life from her like that. Catch up her whole life and take it back. No. "Oh, George," she said, "but we—"

"I know," he said. "I know, Lucy. I was too damned rough for you." And he was crying too, almost, then laughing— A drunk's laugh. Uncle— Then grinning, grinning, holding her right hand— The pink sack on his knees now— Grinning. "Not an old man yet, huh? Firefighting," he said, thumping his chest. "In Nenana." Grinning—

Still crying, she— "At fifty-six? Firefighting, George?" He, too, fifty-six—firefighting. "Oh, George," she said, "you—"

Skin

"No, no," he said. "We, Lucy. We. We still have it." Then: "Drink your beer, Lucy." And he, curling her fingers around the cold wet— With his fingers—

"I don't want any beer, George—" Her glass on the table. There. And the skins, yes— Back on her lap, yes. Safe. The plastic crackle— He patting her both hands— Holding them, holding— "George, I—"

"Yes," he said. "Yes, Lucy, we still—"

"No," she said. "No, George, I've got to—"

Grinning, grinning— "Yes—"

"I'm married, George, and my life has been—"

"Yes," he said. "I know. I can see that, Lucy." That laugh again, then grinning, grinning, holding her both hands. "I can see—" Then, suddenly: "By Christ, you're a white woman, Lucy!" Like a shaman speaking, in him, George— But no shaman, George. Him laughing again, that laugh like a cough— Uncle—

"No, George, I—" But that laugh again—

"Yes, Lucy, a white woman! And still my Lucy," more softly now, patting her both hands with his. "Still prissy—" And that laugh— "You're a prissy white woman now, Lucy."

And: "George!" She, yes— That slap. The sound. Her own fingers tingling, and— Even in the darkness, the beery half-light of that ugly bar— Yes, red. Her own hand's mark there bright against his cheek. Red, red, her own hand's mark—

All the way to the parking lot, through her tears, Lucy could still see it. Even when she leaned, hot, with both hands and her forehead pressed against the searing white metal of the Lincoln's perfect paint. That ache in her throat now and sobbing. Yes— She could still see that spot, bright against his cheek like a scrap of red fox skin.

64

Distance

"Here the earth, as if to prove its immensity, empties itself."

William Least Heat Moon,
Blue Highways

Greta balanced the cigarette between her lips, holding the sweet smoke in her lungs as long as she could while she bent over the fire pit and the smoke-blackened caldron. Behind her the dogs were alert, most of them standing on the roofs of their houses there at the edge of the woods, watching while she poured in the powdered milk, the corn meal, more water, then the broken hunks of dried salmon. The pebbles of IAMs bought in town last week would come last; for now, she had to stir, stir, stir some more, while the dogs started up their caroling, knowing the scent of their supper.

She always enjoyed this, the caldron and the stirring, the mild frenzy of the dogs, the time of year too, with its spirit of endings and the rotted-flesh stink of high-bush cranberries filling the air before the pot began to simmer. But most of all she enjoyed the motion of her arms and shoulders and waist, her thighs and her knees, the beauty of the broom handle swirling its way through the mush to create Oregon, Idaho, Washing-

65

ton, then Alaska—never Canada or California—which she'd prefer to regard as foreign lands, though she only knew California.

And here was her own Salcha now, hers and Chick's and the girls', the river whose music she swayed to, its song hiccoughing behind her, *real*, a low gurgling tune amidst all the noises in the yard, but audible, possessive, the thing that defined this distant place she called home more truly and completely even than Chick—

Greta lifted her head and puffed again at the cigarette, thinking all this—of Chick, who could be a man here, almost a boy, free, a father and still a lover— Yet, another magic she loved, there it was in the pot now, their own dear Salcha, *tiny*, a dash, a mere swiggle of river moving across the heart of Alaska on the surface of that thick, dissolving map—

And Monica was behind her tugging at her coat, whispering something: "Mama, Mama."

If the words were whispered it was Monica, not Melodie.

Thin, fair, frail-looking Monica—though she was every bit as healthy as Melodie—but with Greta's own long, pale face, her blue-veined eyelids, and that voice that fell sleepily into the wind, meek and slack, as if it came to you, shyly, from a distance. Though they were twins, Melodie was opposite; nothing like Greta, everything like Chick. Everyone said that Melodie was her father in female form—dark and sturdy and vigorous as Chick, and just as self-assured. An Alaskan. They said it with admiration.

About Monica, they were silent, though they sometimes patted her head.

Distance

"I'm stirring, hon." Greta gave that answer to the second or third "Mama." She'd tossed her smoke down immediately, of course, and ground it out carefully with her tennis shoe—the last smoke for the day; she'd promised herself that. Now she was smoothing the silky tangles of hair on the child's neck while she watched tenuous Alaska, then the minuscule vein of the Salcha disappear in the mush. Even Melodie's hair would be opposite—like Chick's—in this fall wind and dampness; it would be stiffened into coarse curls by the very same air that seemed almost to melt Monica's limp, fine, perfectly straight unbraidable sand-colored tresses.

And no one would ever think of Melodie's helmet of curls as "tresses"—a lost word anyhow, though she herself loved it. Loved it *truly*, not only for its sound and meaning, or because it did suit the tattered silk that was Monica's hair, but for its age too, its delicacy like fine old china, and the look of it, the sleek, wavy pattern it made in space—"*tresses*"—a thing no one in Salcha understood, not even if you plied them with smoke.

Only one of the clips that she'd used to fasten Monica's ponytails this morning still dangled on the child's neck, out of place as a plastic leech, defiant when she tried to unclip it. Like her own hair, Monica's was impossible, a nuisance. It would have to be worn straight and lank forever; no choice, the way you dared not say tresses out loud in Salcha.

But she could wear it long and well-brushed, maybe. Someday—someplace. A place where it would not tangle rudely in the breeze as her own was doing now— Someone might love the silkiness of it. And Greta made a C in the mush, for Chick.

67

The air was already sharp with the threat of winter though it was not yet October. When the dogs strained at their stakes, some of them hopping down from the roofs of their houses to lift their heads and make the high-pitched chirping noise at which Chick always yelled his command: "Scramble—" then again, "Scramble, bastards!" which silenced them, you could not only hear the crunch of the leaves they landed and pranced in, but smell the dying of the leaves too. It was a lovely smell, sharp and poignant as the season—

But Monica was mumbling again, shuffling her feet in the dust, tugging at Greta's free hand. "It's Mel, Mama," she said, "*Hurry*—" and Greta thought of the minks. Melodie'd probably let them out again, the kind of thing she always did when Chick was gone, as if, despite her likeness to him, she somehow sensed the frivolity of her father's dreams.

If one of the five got away, Chick would murder her. Or Monica. Not Mel. No, he'd never murder Melodie.

She propped the broom handle against the nearest cottonwood and followed Monica, who was panting. She hadn't noticed that before, that Monica was actually panting.

And she was not leading toward the pens, but running for the river, skirting the patch of marijuana plants beyond the vegetable garden—Greta's plantation, Chick called it—then heading into and through the thin stand of aspens and willows that ran first slightly uphill, then suddenly down, toward the water.

Everything seemed to be happening in slow motion, then too fast, too fast, so that when they reached her—*Melodie!*—Greta could not believe what she saw. Everything seemed impossible—everything—like Melodie's boot, her left boot halfway off her foot—a red-topped black breakup boot identical to Monica's, but standing higher than the rest of her, upended and lifted like a marker in the mud—

And Melodie herself so motionless—wet—impossible, for it meant that she'd been in the water, and the girls *knew* they could not go near the water—

But Monica was yelping that she'd pulled Melodie up the bank, out of the water— Out of—

By her boot, then—

But it was *impossible*, all impossible, even to imagine it, as impossible as the limpness and coldness of Mel's legs when she touched them and the flat stillness of her bottom while Greta heard her own voice as if from a distance mouthing words: "Mel, Mel. Please *get up*, Melodie—"

Greta could not hear the song of the river now, or her own panting noise like wind moaning, or the howls of the dogs, or even the remarkable tangled sounds of Monica's bubbly cries: "Mama—Mama—oh, Mel—" and again, "oh, no, Mel," while Greta lifted Melodie from the mud and turned her bluish face up.

She was hearing something else, like the sound of the ocean in the bay at Monterey in her ears, a pounding like her own voice when she'd yelled at Chick, five years ago, there at her grandparents' beach house, that she hated him.

That he was mean, heartless, *wicked*—until he'd laughed and laughed, and hugged her and hugged her again— "So you've got some spit after all," he'd said, and then they'd come, together, gradually, here.

And she'd thought her fury had caused it all—this wondrous distance achieved then overcome; the bravery they'd needed to travel so far together, into this land whose very extremity was the thing she loved and wanted. That distance.

But of course the point was that this was the way the noise had been in her ears *then* too, hating him, loving him—

An illusion. The sound of her own powerless blood, not the surf, not magic or power then, even then, while the tiny, unformed babies already lay hidden inside the smooth curve of her stomach whether she willed it or not, slowly becoming Melodie and Monica—

Even Mel's fingers were cold, though Greta began rubbing them first, why she could not say. She knew CPR, from the lessons at the volunteer fire station, and she blew and blew herself into Melodie's mouth, pumped and pumped at Mel's wet little chest, doing everything right—and fast after all, despite the smoke— though she knew it was all useless.

Because the other thing she knew, suddenly, was distance. True distance.

And that was what everything came to, of course, all other meanings nothing beside this one. The power of this one.

Yes, she was panting now rather than moaning, Monica sobbing there on the bank behind her and the dogs making their mournful yowls—with Chick surely off at a bar in Delta, though he was supposed to be buying roofing shingles for the cabin, and her own mind pulled taut and powerful at last—

Wrenched from its play of smells and fingerings and shapes—wordless, soundless—into this new place that was death.

Everything would be different now, though even as she thought it she could feel that fact receding too, slipping away like her smoke, like the dissolved maps in the caldron or the old sad music from the river, while her fingers still rubbed and rubbed at Melodie's cold wrists and she whispered it over and over: "Melodie, honey. Oh, *please*, honey. *Mel—*"

So this was the real distance then, Melodie gone forever into a place where not she or Monica or Chick or even the river could ever reach her again.

Ruth

"Why do they break all those bottles?" says Ruth. "Having fun's one thing, but who needs that stuff? God! It's—littering." Her words slip through the dry, steady thunder of rock'n'roll and that fluid, bantering noise of voices in a crowd. She sits between Eleanor and me on the curb, her thin knees spread slightly, her hands centered above them to cup a brown, stubby beer bottle.

Ruth is an Athabaskan Indian, but her flat, small-featured face always looks Eskimo to me. It is a pale, bas-relief face, not yet middle-aged, its delicate sculpture darkened by the quick angles of her eyes. Her hair is glossy and black, coarse, marked with faint brown highlights like striations on dark stone. But today— the 4th of July in Seward, Alaska—her hair is barely visible, pulled back from her face into a ponytail, then covered with a red bandanna kerchief so that only wisps and hairline show. Like a set of mismatched triplets, Eleanor and I are also wearing bandannas. Each of us is in jeans. We lift and turn our heads in unison too, sedate as tennis spectators watching two more brown bottles arc slowly through the air, then explode in silent splinters on a square of pavement.

"Two dead Indians!"

73

Ruth

The shout is clear—high-pitched and boyish, coming from somewhere behind us and to the left. Ruth's head dips, her thin shoulders pivot toward the sound. "Bullshit—" she hisses. "You can't kill 'em off so easy as that."

"It's getting wild," Eleanor says. She drinks from her beer, then touches her mouth and chin delicately with a kleenex, so that small red marks come away on the tissue.

Today, I am thinking, is surely the biggest holiday of this swollen Pipeline summer, 1975. And until now, I've only seen Seward in its ordinary state—which is peaceful and sleepy, almost elegiac, slow and tranquil and nostalgically old-fashioned as any storybook city. In fact, I usually think of the town as a down-at-heel Land of Counterpane, nestled carelessly at the base of these fat mountains like a toy city filling the lap of some huge, dozing child. But perhaps Robert Louis Stevenson was "a romantic," as someone told me once; and my maternal, summer-tourist's appropriation of the image in his *Garden of Verses* may be no more applicable to the real Seward than is this wild and summery day.

Beside me, Ruth's weight shifts. She is sipping at her beer, and I decide that today in Seward is distinctly different: my metaphoric child seems awake and angry, about to have a tantrum. Even the sunny perfection of the weather has thickened into an intense, bright heat that shimmers and pulses, pushes against my flesh, surging like the crowd after the Independence Day parade.

The footrace up and down Mount Marathon has ended, but we watch a late finisher—a young female— jog a path through the throngs of people in the street.

74

Her cheeks are flushed under their tan, her chest heaves for breath, and the sides and backs of her legs and track pants are covered with a thin coating of rusty earth. Her hair is damp and matted too, and one elbow looks bloody. A cloth square bearing the number 8 flutters on the back of her t-shirt, and a few hoots, then scatterings of applause break out in the crowd. Ruth, Eleanor, and I clap loudly. Someone whoops, and there is a shout of: "Good goin', man!"

"Man—?" says Eleanor to no one in particular, and we hear a ripple of laughter in the crowd. The runner nods, gives us all a tired and slow stretching of her lips—almost a smile—and waves.

Downhill, young boys tear apart an abandoned parade float. They wrap themselves in crepe paper streamers, light firecrackers and toss cherry bombs onto the newly-exposed, skeletal base of the truckbed. Two of them pitch more beer bottles. Ruth begins to remove her sweatshirt, and music from a loud-speaker at the foot of the hilly street blares and thumps a new tune into the air, syncopating rhythms within the chaos of noise and heat. Snake dancers thread their way around the floats, avoiding the boys, moving clumsily between the crush of street vendors and spectators.

"Look at those hippies!" Ruth half stands and points, flapping her sweatshirt toward the snake dancers. A long-haired couple appear to be copulating in the center of a circle now formed by the dancers. Eleanor covers her mouth with both small hands. Her face muscles are contracting and one eyelid twitches. "Yuk!" she says.

I probably look uncomfortable too, I think. We three are "of an age," as my Grandma used to say, and it is not the correct one for this day or this crowd. Our birthdays, totalled, would number well over one hundred years and, thinking of that, I shiver a little.

"God," says Ruth, as if reading my thoughts. "All this—I feel like an old lady." She places her bottle on the pavement between her tennis shoes.

"You—" Eleanor says with a snort. "I'm thirty-six next week," and she brushes, swats at a mosquito, but misses. Ruth lifts her beer again and sips.

A slender, barely-mature boy in mountaineer boots has climbed the brick and stone front of a bar and hangs from an over-sized neon U, his knees glinting white in the sun. He spreads his arms, dips and lifts his head like a circus acrobat. Whimsically shabby and shaggy young people gather below him to applaud, laugh, shout encouragement. A blond, bearded boy with a kinky ponytail waves his t-shirt, thumps his bare chest, yodels, then yells: "Hang in there, Tarzan!"

On the sidewalk across from us, a fist-fight has broken out. A barefoot girl dressed in the ankle-length tatters of a beautiful quilted skirt stands behind the fighters, vomiting slowly onto the cement. Ruth points again, and the couple at the center of the snake dancers descends toward the pavement, moving at an angle and almost in slow motion to disappear from our view.

"Lord," I say. "I had no idea it would get like this."

Eleanor giggles and leans across Ruth to pinch my shoulder. "Not like old Fairbanks, huh?" For nearly four years, she and Bernie—my husband Ed's younger brother—have been trying to persuade Ed, the kids, and me to sell our home in Fairbanks and move to Anchorage.

"Cripes, Eleanor, not like Anchorage either," says Ruth. She and Eleanor are long-time neighbors there. "Somebody's gonna get hurt!" As if in answer, another beer bottle arcs, then splinters in the street just two feet in front of us.

We are all standing now. "Maybe we should leave," I say.

"They're trying to tell us something!" giggles Eleanor.

"Leave! Not yet," says Ruth. "God, I can't be so old and square to have to leave!" She winks at me. "Just think. Michael told me to wear a dress here when I asked him! A dress!" She pulls her face into a shape that seems to intend an imitation of Michael, who is her second husband, the father of the two youngest of her five children. "Can't you just see me, in this crowd? Whenever I ask him what to wear, he says, 'A dress.' And heels. He loves for me to wear heels. Wouldn't I stand out here, in my taffeta and spikies? Laa-de-daa!"

We all giggle and butt shoulders like schoolgirls, but I am beginning to long for the safety of our tent (Ed's and mine, for we are vacationing without the kids for once) pitched beside Eleanor and Bernie's travel trailer, a mile or so below us on the beach shingle. As we re-settle on the curb, I notice that I am the only one of the three of us to have carried a purse. (A purse!) And I am suddenly aware of my own dizziness, a heady combination of midday heat and beer.

"Men can be so damn strange," says Ruth.

"Especially husbands," I say. "They're so inconsistent sometimes." I hear the hiss of my own slurred S's and think self-consciously again of my purse—and of the impact of this heat and the beer. I wonder if Ruth and Eleanor are feeling as disoriented as I am.

"Oh, I never ask Bernie *a thing* anymore," says Eleanor pedantically. She shifts her fair Botticellian flesh on the curb. And it occurs to me suddenly that her innocent pink body seems to have been shaped by that same intellectual virginity, the same childishly frank and simple process that usually builds her thoughts. I've always felt a certain affinity for physiognomy, I decide beerily, and not much of what I've observed of human behavior in my thirty-five years has shaken this.

Eleanor is continuing, her voice taking on a certain stylization, a faintly contrived but thoroughly familiar lilt. "Not thing one do I ask. Half the time he's traveling anyhow, for the firm. Just gone. But goo-bye, Bernie; hello, freedom. That's my motto now. That's why it's so great to have this dealership. Income! With your own income, you girls could do just what you please, too!" Eleanor pulls off her yellow silk bandanna. She shakes her head dramatically and pats at the sudden fluff of red curls with one small, dimpled child's hand.

"God, it's getting hot here," I say, dreading the possibility that Eleanor, a recent convert to the joys of home-cleansing-aid sales, will again begin a monologue of financial theory. This morning's parade was punctuated by Eleanor's lectures on the Free Enterprise system.

Beside me, Ruth's shoulders draw up stiffly. "Well, I've had income and no income, Eleanor. But the world never changed any on my accounts. Not the women in it. Not the men in it either. Sure as hell not Michael." She sniffs audibly. "I mean, God, Eleanor. That's what there is about Michael, you know? Or your Bernie. That he's no feather to the wind."

"Oh, you," says Eleanor.

But Ruth's voice is continuing, careless but certain, I think, like the small sailboat I can see above the heads of the crowd, skimming the white-spangled surface of Resurrection Bay as I sip from my lukewarm beer and cradle my purse between my hiking shoes. "It's like I told Tessie-my-daughter. Be a good wife, try to be a good person. It means a lot, sure. But, hell, life's not one simple thing. Freedom?" Ruth shakes her head. "I don't mean no damn stuff about incomes."

I know that Ruth's oldest child is nineteen and a young bride moved recently to Valdez, the summer's most apparent boomtown. "How's Tessie doing?" I ask, peeling at the label on my bottle.

"Well, she's been so lonely," Ruth says. She pats my knee, then lifts her beer and sips. "No job yet. She thinks maybe she's pregnant, too. Bill works those double shifts, he's out of town a lot, and she hasn't got *any* friends there. Damn. That damn Pipeline. Big money but bad news." Ruth has exhaled, elbowing Eleanor on the word money. "So, I told Tessie, there's no need to be—you know—a *mortar*. Don't hang around the place sniveling. Nothing like that. Just go out yourself sometimes, girl. Alone if you need to. Freedom, Eleanor?" Ruth winks at Eleanor (who sniffs loudly) then nods to me. "Go to a movie. Or go have a damn beer if you want it. That's what I told her. You just got to keep your own spirit up, you know. You're no good to nobody otherwise." Ruth shakes her head emphatically.

A police car inches through the crowd. The young bodies in the street part slowly—almost like a miracle on the Red Sea, I think—to permit its passage. As the car reaches us, I see that the two patrolmen are smiling, trying to stare straight ahead with faces that have already yielded to the impiety of those faint, testy grins. The young man hanging from the neon U yodels loudly, then waves to them. A beer bottle arcs and crashes against a rear fender of the patrol car, but the vehicle continues to roll steadily forward.

"My God," says Eleanor.

Ruth ignores all this. "Well, Tessie phoned me that she did it. Went out by herself. To a damn bar. First time ever. Bill was out of town again, so— That's about all there is there, Tessie says—bars. Anyhow, she sits down at a table, orders her a beer, and this girl comes right up to her. 'Do you have a pimp?' asks this girl. Bold like brass!" Ruth narrows her eyes, looks into my face. "Tessie gets mad. 'Hell, no!' she says to the girl. 'I'm no whore. I'm a nice girl. I'm married. I've got a mother and everything!' "

Eleanor grimaces, makes a sound between choking and a chuckle. I feel the small muscles at the corners of my mouth begin to ache.

Ruth closes her eyes, nods. "It's true. Tessie told me. The girl says, 'Well, I've got a mother, too!' This girl is kind of insulted, you know? Kind of mad. 'Besides, I just wanted to help you out, kid,' she tells Tessie. 'See, you can't work on your own here. These pimps get together. They'll find out, and they'll beat you up. I've seen girls beat pretty bad.' That's what she told Tessie! It's true! That's it! It made Tessie vomit. My Tessie. That's what she told me on the phone."

Eleanor shudders. "My God," I say.

"Isn't that terrible?" Ruth's pale face is spotted with color now. "They beat those poor girls up. Not that I can think much of those girls. But, God—that! Don't those girls have enough trouble?"

"God!" I say again, ignoring the repetitiousness of the word as I watch Eleanor squirm through what appears to be another shudder.

"But those girls do make a heck of a lot of money, Ruth," says Eleanor in a barely-recovered voice.

"They earn it!" Ruth's face is a solid, deep pink now. "And hell—what does that mean, Eleanor, anyway? Money—?"

We are all silent for a second. Then Ruth continues in a burst of words. "Money? It's—life, Eleanor, damn it. Not just money. Something inside. I don't admire them any, those girls. Hell, they're whores. But you can't hide your head from that stuff either. That's what I told Tessie. And how can *I* say anything about those girls, you know? Hell. Everybody has got to live in the world. But nobody's free just by money, Eleanor. Nobody.

"Like, last week?" Ruth's voice is urgent now. "I heard—my aunt, see? She's in the hospital, you know? Diphtheria is what they said. Diphtheria. Bet you two thought nobody got that, huh? Anymore? Well, you know, she's an old lady. An alcoholic. Had TB once. All that stuff." Ruth lifts and drops her shoulders philosophically. "Well, she grew up in a village. They didn't have diphtheria shots back in those days. She's an old lady anyhow, you know? Half dead, even before the diphtheria. One lung. And the first thing I think is, 'Damn! I don't want to go see her! I might get it!' She's in the Anchorage Native Hospital, you know?

"So, my father writes me: 'Go see her.' And I think again about getting diphtheria. Besides, I say to myself, I probably wouldn't see her if she was just here in town on a drunk. In Anchorage, I mean. But what do I do? I go. Of course—"

81

"Yes," says Eleanor, nodding.

"Well, she's—out of it, you know? Just barely awake. Hell. I don't even know whether she knew me." Ruth pats my knee again. "But I was glad I went. After. Of course—

"Because it was like maybe I owe it to her to go. To see the way she has been a person, you know? Still— it meant nothing. Just life, Eleanor. You got to take your own chances, sure. For yourself, yes! But remember other people do that too, maybe. That's freedom to me. But incomes? Money? Shit—"

Eleanor stands, dusts the seat of her jeans with one pink hand. Her face has a slight, pouty frown. "Oh, you!" she says to Ruth. A beer bottle dips past Eleanor, misses Ruth's head by a fraction of an inch, and shatters on the sidewalk behind us. We're all three on our feet now, and I think rather desperately of our three husbands, out together someplace in this crowd. "Let's go," I say. "Let's get out of here."

Ruth scratches a spot on her bandanna, as if the spot has been grazed by the bottle, though I know that it has not. She looks hard into my eyes, grins, shakes her head. "You go," she says, "if you want to. But remember, it's 4th of July!"

Placing her bottle carefully on the curb, Eleanor leans forward and claps both hands around another mosquito. But when she opens her hands, we see that the mosquito has survived in some small pocket of air caught between her palms. We watch its fragile, ugly form lift slowly and fly away.

Waves

"Hast thou entered into the springs of the sea?"

Job 38:16

1: Breath

She's around him for a few minutes, and she's mouth breathing. Like a fish out of water. As if she can't get enough air to her brain.

2: Air

Air is the thing, in a way, though they've never admitted that. Time isn't in it. There's no chronology to it. She met Bill, yes, on a day or an evening, once, yes, but none of that matters.

"You know what matters." He said that to her once. Those were his words. Nothing to do with air.

Yes, they both know what matters.

3: Love

There's an overhang above the bar. It's squared off, angular, covered in black vinyl, yet it looks like a wave advancing. Bill looks up at it while he talks. He holds

83

her hand, kisses it, presses her wrist to his chest sometimes. When she tells him she loves counseling Natives,
loves to be around them, at the jail where she's working then, her first counseling job, he says, "Well, when
you get over *that*—"

And he grins into her eyes until she looks away to
stare up at the overhang too, trying to find among all
the tiny white electric bulbs glowing like artificial stars
trapped in the padded vinyl the exact point of light
that has just claimed his eyes. Even with her face averted
like this, she can smell his body, his skin and hair and
his breath, a tart, bitter hint of cigarettes and coffee
that she loves, and her fingers draw tight against his
hand while she tries to suck in air; tries, unobtrusively;
mouth breathing again, of course.

The place is called the Wheelhouse. She thinks that's
because the original structure was an old beached river-
boat. It burned down back in the early '70s, before
any Pipeline money started to flow in Alaska, and most
people say the fire was an insurance scam, a planned
fire. But she and Bill won't talk about that, though
he'd know the history of the place—which is concrete
block in this incarnation and painted yellow—it being,
once, his place. Not that he owned it, "just supported
it, kept it afloat." That's what he'd say, probably; yes,
he'd probably say that.

But maybe not. Helen can and can't predict what
he'd say or do in any given situation. But she tries that
less often now, this year, last, the year before, since
he lives in Ketchikan now, not here in Fairbanks.

And she wouldn't have predicted Ketchikan. Not
what he says next either: "The water flows there all
winter." Her Bill, a poet for her, he says that; softly,

84

unpredictably, describing Ketchikan while he squeezes her hand like a sponge.

4: Truth

It's summer 1983, June, midnight, and though it's dusk inside the Wheelhouse, it's still completely light outdoors, broad daylight. And Bill no longer claims this dingy light as he once must have claimed it—she can feel that much. But of course he still claims her without trying. Though the fact that she's here at all is an accident really, despite his phone call. Something a bit like drowning; a thing nobody ever expects to happen.

If he is here by plan, even. Here, lounging, nights, at the Wheelhouse for the whole summer by plan. Here in his home town, Fairbanks, for as long as the season lasts, fighting forest fires for the state, his twenty-third summer of that, as he has already told her twice, and proudly: "My annual God-damned conflagration of trees," but on paper this year. Winters—fall and spring too, though it's winter that matters anyplace in Alaska—he teaches in Ketchikan, as a substitute teacher in the high schools since his job here, doing legal and historical research for the university, "evaporated."

And she's been married for twenty-three years to someone else, but she says it again: "I love you," while his eyes glow and he spreads the fingers of her hand to press her palm to his chest. It's the only thing she can say to him all evening: "I love you. I'll always love you. I love you as much as I've ever loved anyone, even my kids. I want you to know that, to have it, to

85

remember it always—" And she doesn't know why she says it exactly, except that it's true.

He asks her why she's wearing "preppie clothes"— a cotton madras blazer she loves over a t-shirt, with polyester slacks. "Corduroy," he says, his voice profound. "Don't you remember? Corduroy—"

He does not kiss her. But later he'll tell her she's rigid.

"I *knew* you'd say that," she'll say. "I knew you'd tell me that!" And it's true, she did know; just as she knows its all hopeless. Or beyond hope. Everything they do together, beyond hope; beside the point somehow, since only a certain truth that they both know— and both choose to ignore—can exist between them. And that exists permanently.

5: Hope

But hopeless or not, she goes on with it anyway. Not swimming exactly, but drowning in air maybe; flailing, gasping, her own mad attempt at chronology, at history, at truth, here in the Wheelhouse; at breath, June 1983:

"But you're not rigid, are you—?" Just a drunk; she thinks of saying that, wants to say it maybe, but can't since she knows that he knows she thinking it, "—and I love you—" while he grins again and slowly kisses her hands, each in their turn, knowingly, lovingly, drunkenly.

It's the reason she came here probably, to tell him again that she loves him while he drinks black coffee given to him by the tall, beautiful, surly young female bartender, and she sips at Coke thinned by ice, staring up at that vinyl wave and its fake glass stars—just a

shelf designed to hold liquor: It's so good to see you
again. You look well, you look good. It's so good to
see you. I love you. I love you. I love you.

6: Refusals

She has never learned to swim.

In the summer of her tenth year, when she was still
nine, she tried to learn. She tried and tried, the water
claiming her breath each time; the water cold, terrible,
death in it maybe or something worse, some finality
worse than death—

While all around her her friends—Sue Ann, Patsy,
Marlene—learned to swim, she wrapped her skinny
arms around herself and stood in the heat of the Ohio
sun, shivering there at the Milford City Pool. She let
her teeth chatter and went stiff every time somebody
tried to help her, to hold her, to keep her afloat; and
she did not, ever, learn to swim.

That was 1950.

7: Marriage

Would she marry Bill if he didn't drink?

She can't say, but she probably married her husband
because they both love rivers. The only other thing
her husband loves is planes. She can measure their life
together in planes: 1959 was his uncle's Lockheed Vega,
made of plywood, almost an antique, with a Wasp
engine on which he learned the trade; 1961 was a Fair-
child 71 his uncle bought to replace the Vega when it
burned in a hangar fire; 1965 was the Cessna 180 her
husband's parents loaned them the money to buy, his
first plane and the only one he enjoyed flying as much

as repairing—the plane they flew north in; 1969 was the Cessna 185 he bought a share in after he sold the 180. He flew it only once or twice before one of his partners cracked it up on a hunting trip near Paxson—

The others are harder to name, though more recent—two or three Super Cubs, another old Cessna 180, an ancient Stinson that sat in the yard for years waiting to be restored.

It's a kind of history.

8: Rivers

Rivers are a history too. She and her husband made love for the first time beside the Little Miami in Milford, Ohio—which ran near his uncle's hangar and shop, at the edge of the old airport. The night was so humid it took her breath away. Maybe if she'd been breathing things would have worked out differently; she used to joke about that to her husband in the first years of their marriage.

Anyway, two months later they were married and beginning their gradual series of hops west, then north, out of Milford, her husband working for a month or a year in airports along the way. When he bought the first Cessna 180, they flew toward Alaska by following rivers. Then, in Canada, it was the Alaska Highway, like the longest and driest river of all, snaking for days below them. They arrived in Fairbanks in May 1967, though it was pure chance that the house they found to rent, for themselves and their two young daughters, was one block from the slough, the Chena, a small river which runs right through the center of town.

When a housing shortage came along that summer, they decided, on a whim, to buy the house, her husband liking his new job as a mechanic for Wien, servicing mostly bush planes, float planes—though she still thought of their presence in Alaska as a temporary swerve off course; another whim, a fluke, a pause in their real life—an adventure—and they bought the house they'd been renting.

It was a small house close to the airport, in walking distance, in a part of town everybody called Wienville because nearly all the adults who lived there worked for Wien or else for Alaska (they called it "Elastic") Air. The house had a pretty yard, and the woods behind it led right down to the banks of the Chena. They made their first mortgage payment on the first day of August 1967, and later that month a hundred-years' flood came, pouring five feet of water through the house, floating the living room furniture out through the broken picture window, collapsing the bed and the TV stand, the chests of drawers, the bookcases—leaving water behind everywhere.

Water, then mud. Afterwards, mud. Velvety swirls of mud like waves on the walls and kitchen table; leaf embroidery, in mud, on the kitchen counters, the beds, the lampshades, the carpets, the bathroom and kitchen sinks. She remembers that the swirls of mud seemed fine as new snow, lacy or velvet-looking, like etchings designed by the water, delicate rivulets of silt left behind by the Chena. So beautiful—

Because the funny thing was that she loved that house anyway, its location and the river. She loved being perched there on the bank to gaze down at the tan and gray-green water—a capricious foe, a lover which frightened her and her husband several times afterward, after The Great Flood, but never again flooded.

She loved it there.

She and her husband cleaned and dried each room and carpet, threw away the furniture, books, toys, ruined clothes, and her husband even sold the Cessna 180 rather than take out a government loan. They continued to live there till long after they'd outgrown the house—for eighteen years, in fact, and yes, the truth was she loved it.

9: Swimming

Like her father, Helen's oldest daughter, Marcie, swims easily. She moves away into the fog of steam at the hot springs pool, sinking then rising, full-grown, disappearing. Helen stands in the four-foot water, in the five-foot—no deeper—and she loves these hot waters, the Chena's source. She pushes off again and again from the slimy side of the pool, hoping to swim, pretending to swim, trying. Thinking of Bill, she breathes this steam—sulphurous—

Yet a wonderful gift too, *summer* here in this enchanted place that holds heat in the middle of winter, minus thirty degrees outside. It's 1985, she's now a grandmother, and she has not seen Bill, except for that time in '83, since he moved to Ketchikan. She pushes off again and again, but she doesn't swim. Even in this hot mineral-thick soup in which no one would expect to drown, hardly anyone even fail to float, no, she cannot swim.

A person could drown, she guesses, but only by accident; only by bumping her head or being overcome by the heat; something "accidental" like that. And she's not really afraid of drowning; it's just that she can't possibly swim.

The sides of the pool are draped in plastic sheeting that's covered with small turquoise and gold abstract designs, plus a faint tracery, almost a trim, of mold. The sheeting looks like an old shower curtain, a relic from the '50s or '60s, but the hot springs pool is wonderful nonetheless. It's February; the greenhouse windows that enclose the pool are wet with vapor that's frozen in splotches, large caky blobs of white hoarfrost; and beyond the window the yard is thick with two or three feet of snow. Frost hangs in veils and sheets from all the branches of all the trees; huge icicles dangle from the roof, then swell magically when they near the ground, becoming drip hills, dwarf mountains, pearly globs that rise, deformed and luminous, beyond the steamy windows.

Her daughter appears again and swims toward her in the fog. She's beautiful—a mermaid, a young mother already, impossible to believe that, her approaching face large like her father's, but beautiful, her daughter's breasts so much riper than her own—

As if she can read minds, Marcie laughs, reaches out, offers to take Helen's hand and lead her into the deeper water. "You'll learn—" she says.

But Helen shivers, shakes her head, whispers, "No thanks." She doesn't know for certain whether or not she bothers to say the rest of it: "I'm hopeless." Because she knows it then. For the first time, she knows it. The truth. That she already lives water, a life that's unknown to those who merely swim.

10: Fate

"You're a fatalist." Bill said that to her once, staring at her, saying it flatly, incredulous, the way she tells him she loves him.

She began to laugh, to cry, to unbraid her hair—which she cut the next day—leaning across the desk in this office to unbraid it.

"No, no, a *realist*," she said. "And you. You're a history teacher." Which he was that semester, part-time.

11: Reality

That's what she knows nothing about maybe, reality, though she tries to know it. It's the reason she decided to study counseling; the thing that makes her such a good counselor probably, such a sympathetic listener, so compassionate, so tender and patient. "What would you like to be doing with your life, *really*?" She can say it and no one ever feels intimidated; maybe because they sense that she knows nothing about life, nothing about anything but feelings, nothing at all about "reality."

And of course it's the complaint everyone who knows her well has made to her always too, all her life, all the time—her parents, her children, her husband, even Bill: "But Helen (or Mother), be *realistic*." She's rigid in her refusals, too, and stubborn; they all imply that.

Once, in 1979 or 1980, trying to "be realistic," she sat down and wrote two lists. It was a counseling method she'd just studied, but she changed things a bit. One list was her husband; the other was Bill.

A large head, large hands, that was her husband. Bill was his neat small head not yet going bald, his hands no larger than her own but harder, his lips soft and kind as a woman's. Bill was talk of William James and streams of consciousness, the river of time; Bill was quotes from Heraclitus and Bergson, *l'experience vecu*, words that made her head swim.

Bill was eyes that played with hers or, sometimes, worshipped; a voice amazingly rich and deep for someone who wasn't tall. Talk, talk, talk, jokes always, even while he made love—or at least the one time they'd tried it—that was Bill.

Her husband was silence—his eyes, his slow-moving body, his large wide mouth centered above his big jawline. His head was a brooding head, like a bull's, and when she talked too much, he told her she was "going off the deep end again." And then the silence in his eyes was fiery. Talk seemed to insult him, as silence could hurt or arouse Bill.

If Bill was play, always, everywhere—and water, yes, "whiskey and water," he'd say, even his voice rich and playful, like the noise of a brook—then her husband was business and weight, always, and silence, and yes, *heat*—his big body heavy atop hers, his lovemaking fast and hard and staunch, his shoulders blocking the view and his face looking the way it had those hot evenings when he'd worked on planes in the first years they were married. She'd loved to sit on the tarmac below him then, in the fading evening light, basking in the stored heat from the sun and watching his face— the heavy, still fret of his face.

She hadn't meant to love Bill, of course. It was strange that she had. What she'd meant to do was go back to school to find herself—another strange idea, of course.

Strange too to think that her husband was a pilot, since nothing about him made her think of air. Everything about him was thickness and weight—though of course he preferred to see himself as a mechanic, pre-

ferred to work on planes, not fly them. When he flew—
like the long trip with their daughters when they moved
to Fairbanks—he planned every step of the flight for
weeks in advance as if he were plotting a war (so unlike
Bill, who never planned anything)— As if she and the
baby girls were his troops on that long trip, and the
air that carried them was his enemy—

Just as water seemed to be hers, maybe.

Yes, water, her enemy, yet something she loved—

And she was crumpling the lists, tearing them up—

12: Being

She still writes various things to Bill sometimes;
sometimes even mails them. Letters, journal entries,
notes—not just from her heart but from her being—
no longer the history papers she so lovingly composed
when she was his student, making his eyes go soft, his
brown eyes dense and dark as alluvial mud then—

Yes, she was his housewife student, dressed in old
warm boots every day, fall, winter, or spring—never
summer then—and corduroy slacks. No makeup, no
tight sweaters (silly on her small breasts anyhow),
sturdy boots, pale braids, and no frills, *ever*.

She would *not* be one of the skirts chased by the
handsome, young, newly divorced professor; the visiting professor, "on loan," as he'd said once to her
class, "from history and the law."

She *would not*, would *not*, would not—

She would not be anything except what she was—
what she *is*—his. His woman. The one made for him,
born for him, exactly right in mind and body and soul
for him. Her hair in pigtails, then cut off. Straight. No
frills, no frills, no frills ever, dammit. He will love her

94

as she is or not at all, warm boots, corduroy jeans, history papers rather than love words then, 1978—

He doesn't answer—or grade—the things she writes anymore, her letters in the sand as she thinks of them now, in 1988. He only in fact said he loved her so very obliquely then, though he said it. In jokes and metaphors and riddles, all the ways she has tried to remember and then to forget for all these years, but did not ever *need*.

She needs—and needed—nothing. Because she already has it. She already knew it, had already recognized and lived and refused everything even then, 1978, every predictable "reality," long before they'd named it, long before he'd offered it, always—the single fact of her life that proves she is *not* "a fatalist" at all.

And that was because it was all already hers. Reality. Bill's breath her life, her element, her being, the thing she was born for—all other love only practice for this, so what could it matter, exactly, what either of them said or did, ever?

This was the water from which they would not escape.

13: Escape

But then, needing nothing, she didn't *need* to escape.

It's the reason she said yes when Marcie's husband Todd suggested that they all go to the Wheelhouse for another beer. It was after a softball game, a beery game, the last in the season for Marcie and Todd's team from work. Anyway, she'd been making an effort lately to be more practical, to at least try to see things as others seemed to see them.

She couldn't believe Bill would be there—

But he was, August 1988, drunk, feeding quarters into the juke box. "A different girl," he said, when she managed to excuse herself from her husband and went to stand—a bit unsteadily, maybe—beside him. "Do I know her?"

"A woman," she said, trying to catch her breath while she watched the colored lights in the juke box begin to dissolve and blend. "Not a girl. A grandmother. A friend."

"And not even sober. What's going on here? Are you running away?"

"No, no," she said, "nothing like that," and she'd found his eyes, those eyes she would always love. But, suddenly, staring into them, she knew it was true; she'd never love anybody but Bill, never want or need anyone else, but already it was getting harder to say it.

"What are you doing now?" She could feel her voice growing breathless, the air disappearing from her lungs, that old ache beginning in her throat.

"Just what it looks like," he said. "Care to join me?"

"Getting gloriously drunk." She was whispering it, more breathless now, while she backed toward the restroom. She could see her husband starting to get up, looking toward them, pushing away from the bar and standing; then she'd backed all the way into the restroom and closed the door. She couldn't hear any more of Bill's words through the door, over that noise like sea water in her ears—

It was blood coursing probably, her own blood, but a familiar noise—yes, the sound you must hear while you're drowning.

Hitchhikers

"Well, I'd say he looks about like your ordinary, upstanding citizen of Fairbanks," says my Aunt Louise. She's braking the pickup, rolling down the window and sticking her arm out to signal a lane change, then a left, for a U-turn on the divided highway. Peck stands about a quarter-mile back on my side, on the snowy berm below Birch Hill, near the cemetery, with his right arm raised and his thumb out. He hasn't noticed that the truck's turning, of course. Even when we passed him, his gaze was fixed way beyond us, squinting toward town.

"But Louie," I say, "consider what he did." I'm watching him through the back window while my aunt arranges her turn, and I'm not thinking of blood and gore at all, in spite of my words, but only how amazingly tall he is—probably six-six, though I'd always assumed he was more like six-one or six-two.

Which is ridiculous, because I should be putting my foot down before things have gone too far. I mean, I *know* I ought to be warning Louie, as all the family calls Louise, rather than studying Peck. He's an Alaskan weirdo, I guess—this odd-looking, pasty-faced, skinny guy about my age—thirty-four—and he's famous locally because seven or eight years ago he killed his cousin.

97

But it's not only that that makes him a weirdo. It's not even the obvious physical things—like that lanky, slope-shouldered, plunging walk when you see him hiking through town, or the loony glint to his eyes, which are pale gray, the color of weathered wood, and the way he hides them, with his head down, his chin tucked into the collar of that wornout parka. It's not even the odd sound of his voice—"like an ocarina," Louie will say later—or his solitary ways, but the fact that everybody thinks he must be—

"Half-mad," intones Louie, mumbling to herself. She has that grim look on her face, and she's hunched herself forward, twisting the truck's big steering wheel with all her might. Since January we've been taking afternoon courses together at Tanana Valley Community College—she, a basic computer course "for fun," and me, Child Development while my kindergartner and second grader are in school. I hope to finish my nursery school certification in the next year, by the time the new division moves onto Ft. Wainwright, the local army post. Louie works part-time as a bookkeeper, but that's not why she's studying computers. She has what she calls "aspirations in computer art," though I suspect it's all part of that mandala study business she's been so caught up in lately. But that's another story.

"You'll be the death of us, Louie," I say, but she only grins. Anyway, today does feel like a day for adventure. It's March 20, the first day of spring, though only the dance of sunlight on Louie's cracked windshield hints at the change in seasons, and she's just turned north again and lost that. She's finished her second U-turn by now, and her tires are crunching toward Peck through dry clods of plowed snow.

Peck has put his arm down and started walking toward the truck. It's a yellow 1976 Chevrolet, one of the few Alyeska pickups still around, I guess, ten years after the Pipeline boom, and its backend is loaded with two-by-fours which Louie plans to make into a frame for a greenhouse. She hasn't tried carpentry before, but she's an avid gardener and, as always since she divorced Uncle Martin, no challenge seems too great for Louie. I still haven't adjusted to all this vim and vigor. For instance, I worry about the effect carpentry will have on her back, which has been out of alignment for weeks. Or maybe it's a muscle spasm or something. When she pulled into the driveway at noon to get me, here was tiny Louie bent forward in the cab of the pickup looking as if she might be sniffing the steering wheel.

"Oh, Louie," I finally say—too late, of course—"you *know* we shouldn't. And *I'll* have to sit next to him," for Peck is ambling, with that odd gait of his, over to my side and beginning to open the door.

"Just remember, it was *his father* all along." Louie hisses that in a too-loud whisper as I scoot toward her on the crumbly vinyl. She's leaning forward, extending her right arm across me toward Peck. "I'm Louise Barnes," she says, shaking his raggedy glove, "and this is my niece, Rosalind Lemmert."

Actually, Peck and I went to school together for one year, at Hunter Elementary in about the third or fourth grade—a tidbit I don't intend to deliver to Louie, ever. I'm hoping that Peck—"Austin Peck Junior," his full name, as I know well, and as he is saying now in that high-pitched, strangled-sounding voice while he leans across me to pump Louie's hand—won't remember me. My married name should help, though Peck probably once knew Ted too, and maybe the use of my given name—Rosalind, gads!—will trigger something. Not that many Fairbanksans name children for Shakespeare's characters, I guess, the way Mama did all four of us. Though I happen to know that Peck's younger sister Alma was named by their mother for the woman in Tennessee Williams' *Summer and Smoke.*

But Peck doesn't seem to recognize me. He's concentrating instead on fitting his long body into the cab of the pickup, carefully closing the door. There's an awful smell to him—sweet and fermented, vinegary, spicy, like Chinese food that's gone bad.

"We go as far as the Hot Springs Road," says Louie, which is a lie. Because we both live off Farmers' Loop, its intersection less than a quarter-mile from here, where Louie made her first U-turn. The Hot Springs Road is three or four miles further, straight ahead.

"That'll be fine," answers Austin—Peck, I mean— and I all at once start to see that Louie has caught me in her web again. I mean, I suddenly see that I'm thinking of Peck as *having* a first name, a human history. I'm remembering what a strange boy he was in third or fourth grade, and how some of the kids called him "Aussie"—which he hated, because he said it meant Australian, and his father had told him the settlers of Australia were all convicts. I'm even recalling that he wore a dirty Alaska-flag patch sewn on his coat— roughly sewn, his own big stitches. I was trying to learn to sew too, and I both lusted after that patch and dreaded it a bit, the way you do something in your mind associated with—well, haywires is what Ted calls such people.

"I live a short walk from the Hot Springs Road," he says.

100

And I'm starting to feel really p.o.'d at Louie for doing this. I mean, invading the life of Austin Peck Junior just for a lark, then forcing *me* into it too. I promise myself that I won't say a word to Austin; at least I can distance myself that much from Louie's little game. Still, I'm all at once considering how awful the trial must have been for him. What a nightmare to be pushed even further from other people. Terrible enough that he'd killed someone he probably loved— the one person who'd always stood up for him, for criminy's sake, a cousin who was more like a brother— but then, after that, to have to stand trial for murder!

Now Louie is leaning over me again to chatter as she pulls back out onto the Steese. "First day of spring," she says. "Sunlight sure does look fabulous, doesn't it?" And the plastic-covered photo of Corazon Aquino—Louie made it; it's in a yellow mandala-shaped frame covered with woven yarn, and it dangles by this crocheted chain from Louie's rearview mirror. Anyway, this sacred object of Louie's is flashing sunlight right into Peck's eyes.

He's nodding, holding his body stiff and away from me on the seat. "Sure does," he says in that quavery voice, and he pulls the knit cap from his head so that I'm remembering his hair. I mean, seeing it, I remember it as it was. Odd-colored and beautiful. Then shaved from his head, midway through the school year, though I can't recall ever learning why. When we were in— yes, *third* grade at Hunter School. Amazingly thick, pale hair—that pinkish-gold champagne color older women achieve with dye. It's the same color now, but darker and coarse looking. Maybe that's age, or dirt.

"Looks like summer's not far off," says Louie, her second or third whopper in five minutes. Anyway, I'm

101

recalling the killing, that the quarrel really was, just as Louie hinted, between Peck and his father. The cousin had been away at medical school in Seattle on a scholarship. He was smart, handsome, promising—he'd been raised by Peck's family, and he was the one person, as I said before, who always stood up for Peck no matter what. Well, this time he intervened in the quarrel, stepping into the doorway of the cabin where Peck lived, behind his father's garage out on the Richardson Highway near Birch Lake, where people in Fairbanks own summer cottages— Gads! How all this is flooding back, as if I lived it too!

"I picked up another hitchhiker near here once," Louie is saying now, while I, like Austin, hold my body stiff. I'm trying not to breathe. The smell of him is enough to make a dog barf.

"Two and a half years ago it was," she says, "right across the highway near the A-frame store."

"Umm—" says Austin, or something like that. Maybe, "Humm." It's an amazingly sane answer anyway, considering.

And, yes, I remember it exactly now. The cousin was home from school for Spring break, and he'd driven out to the lake as a surprise on a Friday night. He came with Austin's sister—with Alma and her husband and their new baby. When they arrived, they found Austin Senior angry as usual at his namesake son, and drinking. Everything as usual, except he'd been threatening to shoot Austin, and in fact was already shooting. He'd shot out the window of his son's cabin, as I recall, and Austin's mother was terrified that he'd been shot. She'd even called the State Troopers.

But no Troopers had arrived yet, and he wasn't actually hurt. Instead Peck—Austin—Austin Peck

Junior—was in the cabin terrified. So much so that he'd pulled out his gun brought home from Vietnam—which some people say was the source of all his troubles, Vietnam, though I doubt that—and he was ready to defend himself.

This was about when the cousin and Alma and the rest of them arrived, and shortly after that the Troopers—with sirens, Peck said at his trial. Anyway, it was mass confusion, but somebody—Alma, I think—had managed to take away Austin Senior's gun and talk a bit of sense, while the cousin raced out back to the cabin to see whether Peck had been hurt. Nobody knows why the cousin didn't identify himself, though Alma testified that she thought it was the general panic and confusion, or maybe his loyalty to Peck, which might have made him think Peck would automatically recognize him. I've suddenly thought of the most likely reason—the sirens drowned him out.

Anyway, I have to imagine the rest of it, which is hard to do with Louie chattering and Peck sitting silent and smelly beside me. But I do it; I close my eyes to hear the sirens starting up, and I see Peck crouched below the broken window—he's trembling; I'm sure of that, I can see it clearly. He's pressing the stock to his cheek to steady it, sobbing to himself. I can imagine him hearing voices, loud voices, then sirens, footsteps maybe; then he's lifting the gun and shooting toward the opening door—

But his cousin—not his father—was shot.

Self-defense was the verdict from the jury.

I remember that suddenly too. The jury refused to address the issue of sanity, and Peck was not sent to jail—and not back to API in Anchorage, which is what everybody around here calls Alaska Psychiatric Institute, the state mental hospital, where he'd been sent two or three times before—but released.

"The only other time I ever picked up a hitchhiker," Louie is continuing, while I try to suppress a shudder. "I don't believe in it. But she was so—well, strange, I guess." Louie looks across me as if I'm invisible to say that—honestly, *that!*—to Austin the albino mole, which is what I've heard he was called in high school—Austin Covington Peck Junior. For I can all at once remember that too, his whole name—from the newspapers.

Anyway he doesn't answer that one from Louie, but it doesn't matter because she's going on—without him or me, I'm thinking. "You see, my husband—my former husband Mart—was driving. There was a big sale on beer, and we were going in to town to buy eight cases— our winter supply. Because it was, oh, mid- or late-September, you know, and we—well, it just seemed like a good idea at the time, snow flying soon and all that. Even though we weren't drinkers. Drinking is one thing that doesn't pay in this climate. But I guess you know that already." And Austin is nodding in agreement.

Get on with it, Louie! If you *must* do this, get *on* with it! That's what I'm thinking, and I'm sorely tempted to say exactly those words out loud, despite my promise to myself. But she is, then, finally.

"Well, Mart was driving, so I was the one who saw her, this hitchhiker. I noticed the way she was walking, on the gravel outside the A-frame store—on tiptoe, you see." And Louie nudges me with her elbow as if to say *talk, damn you*, then inclines her head toward Peck again. Toward Austin, I mean.

Damned if I'll say a word, Louie, is what I'm thinking.

"Well, on closer inspection, it turns out the reason the woman is on tiptoe is because she's *barefoot*. A middle-aged lady, fifty-five or so. Ordinary looking, sedate, a bit plump—barefoot. And she's wrapped in a blanket, just like a Plains Indian."

I'm chuckling in spite of myself. Louie has never told me this one before. I can feel the tension going out of Austin's shoulders too, beside me on the seat.

"So, like, I say, *Look, Mart! Stop!* or something, and Mart pulls our truck—not this one—over toward her and I lean out the window. *Can we help you, ma'am*? I say. Something like that. Something polite. Although by then she actually has her thumb stuck out to hitch-hike. Just like you did back there."

Austin is chuckling a bit by now too, because the picture of all this is so clear for him too, I guess. I can see the gold leaves on the birch trees near the dumpster, and the gas pumps, and the evening sun still bright as midday, then the proper-looking middle-aged lady—with a round pink face and grayish-blonde, short hair is how I imagine her—wrapped in a blanket, sticking her thumb out.

"Well, she nods, sedate as can be, still, and she climbs up into the truck. I'm sitting where Rosie is, and I can pretty quick *tell* that she's— Well, this lady is wearing not one stitch of clothing under her blanket, if you see what I mean."

There never were any sex charges that I can think of against Austin, but *nevertheless*— I feel my face going red, both my eyes closing. Gads, Louie, I'm going to get you later for all this, I'm thinking.

"What happened to her clothes?" asks Austin in his strange voice.

105

"That was what we never could figure out. She told us some complicated tale about how they were stolen; happens all the time there, was what she said. She was running a load of laundry in that, quote, 'little laundromat they have there,' taking a shower while the clothes washed, and somebody came in and stole the whole kit and caboodle. Everything!

"She said her husband's camper was broken down out on the Richardson Highway near Delta, and he'd, quote again, 'pay anyone one hundred dollars who'd drive her out there.' No go with us, of course. 100 miles! How she'd got *into* and *beyond* Fairbanks, and why she'd ended up doing her bathing and laundry way out here at the A-frame store was something she never explained.

"Mart suggested that we could drive her to the police station to report the theft, but she turned pale on that one. 'You can let me out here,' she said, which was Gavora Mall. Said a bunch of people there knew her, though she'd lived in recent years in Juneau. But, in the end, we drove her downtown, where she had some nieces and nephews, she said. Tiny little house with rock music playing, cars everyplace." Louie sighs loudly at this point.

"When she got out of the car, she took my hand and squeezed it. 'God bless you,' she said. Odd as it sounds, that blessing changed my life. It made me decide to divorce my husband."

I thought the divorce had been motivated by a pigeon—an injured or confused, disoriented bird that landed on Louie and Martin's deck and stayed for two days. But now I can believe this. Knowing Louie, I can see that this event—followed in a day or two by the pigeon's strange wobblings at the bird feeder on their deck in the suburbs where pigeons are never seen—well, all this had been a clear message for Louie. She'd understood that she finally had to begin to live, as she always puts it, referring to the two years since her divorce, "my real life."

"A strange tale," says Austin, his voice almost warbling.

"Yes," answers Louie, "isn't it though? Stranger yet, I made several trips after that, checking around at the A-frame store and all over the neighborhood, and nobody'd ever *heard* of a laundromat in that vicinity. But the point of it, you see, is that people *can* change. I did, after that."

Austin looks across me at her, me still trying not to breathe, and he says nothing for a second. Then he sort of whistles it: "Some of them."

"Yes," Louie answers. "Some."

"I knew your father once," she says then, "when I was just a girl," which I know is another lie. "Handsomest young man I ever saw," she says, "but a Prussian, next thing to a Nazi. That's what I always thought of him when we were young." Actually, Louie came to Alaska in 1961, as a married woman of 27, married to my mother's younger brother Martin. I can't *believe* she's saying all this! "Looked so much like you," she says, "though he carried the grace differently."

That's exactly what she says. I quote for you: "he carried the grace differently."

Even without turning my head, I can tell that Austin has begun to blush. "Well," he says, "a Prussian. I guess I thought that too, the time he shaved my head for forgetting to burn the trash. Only one way to things, for Dad, and it was never a way I could—manage."

And his voice has that sound again when he says it, "*manage—*" like an ocarina.

"This is it," he says then, suddenly, tapping on the window glass so that I notice we've almost reached Chena Hot Springs Road. "I can walk from here."

Louie is pulling over without any more talking, and Austin leans across me to shake her hand. "God bless you again," he says, opening the door, while Louie smiles back: "Yourself." And I think maybe I'll tell him after all that we went to school together. But when I open my mouth to say it, I find that something or other has come over me. I can't talk. And I'm thinking that even mentioning those times might be a way of acknowledging some terrible distance between us.

Anyway, Austin shakes my hand too, politely, nods, turns on his heel, and walks toward Chena Hot Springs Road with his shoulders hunched down as if they're trying to fight back against that odd, bounding walk of his. I'm wondering whether he lives in some shabby, homey little cabin like Louie's, hidden uphill among the spruce trees. Or maybe there at the trailer court that gets orange, murky mud from the faucets rather than water. I hope he doesn't live in a packing crate like some street people I've seen.

"You did *not* know his father," I say, finding my voice again as I turn toward Louie. "His father is a fat little blonde man who looks *nothing at all* like Austin."

"Rosie," says my Aunt Louise, pulling the truck crookedly back out onto the Steese Highway to begin maneuvering her way into what will eventually become another U-turn, "I believe there are things in this world, child, of which you and I have not even the remotest, faintest inklings."

Fixing Blame

"Why should not we also enjoy an original relation
to the universe?"

Ralph Waldo Emerson, "Nature"

I'd like to fix blame—fault McMullen for good and
all the way Ray's children do. But I know that's just
too easy. Because even the air and the sunlight on that
July evening held certain enormous complexities. Still,
it *is* true that everything started off with McMullen,
with that sudden metallic thud of his truck turning
onto the lane we shared. Then came all those smaller
clanks and rattles and grindings. I looked across my
wheelbarrow, across the clean-smelling mound of
weeds I'd just extracted, and I saw the rusted-out nose
of his pickup rounding the curve, hitting another pot-
hole with an inordinate crash. And it was just as Ray
used to say—like standing witness to an oil slick, or
like blight on wheels.

But that night there was an odd beauty to it too.
Dust rose up in small spiraling clouds beside the truck,
then melted into pale golden light. I thought of coffee
lace, of the fabric of my second wedding dress—how
I'd chosen it in Ft. Worth when Ray and I were about
to head North to be married. Because the dust hung
in the air in just that way, delicate and fragile as veiling.

There was no pinkness to the Fairbanks sun either, though it must have been ten o'clock, and the Delta area burn surely should have brought some haze. Or that bittersweet pinch at the nostrils that would be the smell of forest fire. But there was none. Instead, the air was moist and clean, the way one peal of a silver bell might look, could you see it. A light rain had fallen at midday, and the lawn, my flowerbeds, and the woods beyond the lawn all glistened and glittered with a fine, shimmering clarity.

Even the noise of McMullen's truck welled up into a richness I'd never considered before. The truck was coming closer, misfiring, with its load of old tailpipes, battered oil drums, and ripped-out tire casings bouncing grandly. And that clatter rose forth and took on a structure intricate as a drumbeat, patterned that way and yet somehow wild. I was crouched on my knees in the grass, still weeding, and I leaned toward my arctic poppies, peering through the screen of delphiniums to listen and watch—until I felt my hand tighten on the trowel. I looked away then.

The fact is, I was frightened, suddenly. Because I could no longer see in McMullen's progress that "banality of evil" Ray had always harped on so. Instead I was seeing for the very first time the thing I'd already begun to feel without words. I saw that poor, haphazard McMullen in all his slovenness had somehow managed to achieve—something. A state of grace, it seemed to me that night, and that knowledge frightened me more than anything in the world.

McMullen was about a hundred feet beyond our yard by then, there by the stand of old birches. I dropped the trowel and stood up, stretching into the midnight sun to view the truck's slow, thudding descent into that chaos he called a driveway. And I remember that the sky was that perfect blue color so common to Fairbanks, and that I watched until McMullen and his truck were swallowed whole by our woods, swallowed by the half-acre of willows and cottonwoods that separated his property from ours and made life bearable for Ray. And God knows why, but a cold chill ran through my entire body.

I couldn't go back to gardening. I felt as if I'd already betrayed Ray, and I finally had to pick up my things and roll the wheelbarrow back toward the house and give up. I felt that lost. I dried the trowel and tucked it away in the basket on the storm porch. Even the buttery yellow blooms of my cinquefoil, my favorite wild plant, my sweet, thriving tundra rose, could not cheer me. Ray and I had carried that cinquefoil home in the car from our honeymoon. It was a gray-green twig in a coffee can then, dug wild from the hot, swampy flats beyond Mendeltna Creek. Now small yellow roses bloomed at a height above my knees, and below the yellow blooms were lavender Siberian asters, two wondrously flat-blossomed monkshood, and a cluster of wild delphiniums that hovered like shy, tall maidens among the Iceland poppies. Those flowers had all stood like dearly loved offspring of my feelings for Ray, but that night the sight of them brought vinegar to my tongue.

You see, my husband Ray hated L. T. McMullen. His eyes used to harden and his mouth tense up at the mere mention of the man's name. "By thunder, he *has* a full-time job," he'd say, because we'd learned that McMullen delivered heating oil for one of the local companies. "So why in tarnation the junkyard? I might-could accept some blow of poverty, but this is *point-*

less!" And Ray would slap his palm hard against his thigh as he said it: "*pointless!*"

Ray had been that way ever since we'd moved onto the two acres of land adjoining McMullen's property nearly three years before the night I'm trying to tell about. No, three years less two weeks, because it took Ray two weeks to notice McMullen's place at all. But, when he did notice it, well, everything just seemed to change for him then, some way—our marriage, the property, everything. It was as if McMullen's very existence meant to Ray that some trick or other had been done to him, and to him alone. And the odd thing was that he discovered McMullen's property just when his own riverbank project was beginning.

That started off simply enough, too—idly, casually, almost like aimless beachcombing. Ray had always loved to walk, and the well-drained high bank of the Chena River, which bordered the north end of our property, seemed a perfect place. I even went along at first, chattering away as I walked beside him. Ofttimes I'd be hauling my grandchildren, or his, in the wagon. That is, until I saw that the beachcombing was a solitary pursuit for Ray, maybe even a way for him to pull back from me.

Because we'd started off so swiftly—Ray and I had done, you see—after we met on the plane. On the Alaska Airlines Golden Nugget flight from Seattle—widow and widower seated side by side, each of us coming North for the first time to visit married children.

And I guess the strange thing was the inevitability of it all. Our seating on the plane was the first thing, then it turned out that our children were neighbors. We both loved Alaska on sight—including McKinley as we flew over—and it seemed we were falling in love. That fact hit both of us right off, embarrassing Ray far more than it ever did me.

Because I've never been one to fight against life, and we were both fifty-nine then and lonely; so in a matter of weeks we'd both sold every stick of furniture and vehicle and patch of land we owned in Texas—for Ray lived in Ft. Worth too—and we flew North a second time, together, to be married by the justice of the peace in Fairbanks. Our children loved it—my grown daughters weeping at my wedding, even Ray's sons! And we settled down after that easy and natural as geese migrating for the summer, though it turned out that only I loved the intensity of the winters—

But, anyway, everything did seem a wondrous stroke of good fortune at first. Within two weeks, Ray was working as an accountant again, I'd found a part-time job in a greenhouse, and we'd made the down payment on our pretty little log cabin nestled on a high bank of the Chena. We were both infatuated with that river, you see, with the way it winds and winds through the center of town, cutting Fairbanks into two spiraled halves to be forever crossed and re-crossed by bridges of steel or ice. Perhaps that infatuation was the exact thing that kept us from noticing McMullen's place before we bought the property—who knows how such things happen, just as sweet milk sours.

But I guess I've strayed from the point. Ray had started, in the early walks, by filling his pockets with random rusty nails, battered tin cans, cigarette filters, and bits of broken glass. But soon he was digging up half-buried cans, rolling back rusted-out fifty-gallon oil drums ("the state flower of Alaska," Ray's son John called them), and dragging ever-larger debris to a pile

113

at the far end of our woods, just above the riverbank. He found two rusty gates, many mud-sodden boards, and, once, a nearly antique wringer wash machine. Ray dug at that washer for weeks before he asked me to help. The look on his face then was as close to triumph as I've ever seen it. It still pains me to remember the oddly limited joy in his eyes as we tore that washer like a thorn from the Chena's silty side and rolled it away.

Yet there was more to it, too. During his walks, Ray kept count of what he saw as increasing numbers of wild animals on the banks of the river or in the water. He'd seen sandpipers, Canadian geese, three ptarmigan, four or five spruce hens, several moose, and a beaver that had begun to appear regularly just that summer, and these he attributed to his clearing and cleaning efforts.

So anyway, you can surely understand now why Ray hated McMullen. Besides which, the zoning laws in our borough simply did not prohibit McMullen's hoard of trash, not so long as the stuff stayed within the boundaries of his own property. Ray's petitions to change the zoning laws did no good either, and it appeared that his last legal hope was an antiquated statute related to use of the riverbank. This law said that the narrow strip of land bordering the river could never be privately owned. Land owners adjacent to it could store boats, fish, walk, or beachcomb, but no one could legally build a structure—or deposit personal trash, Ray hoped—on his beloved strip of riverbank.

But during that summer, McMullen's trash piles had edged closer and closer to our property, and to the legal boundary. In fact, before beginning his walk that July evening, Ray had told me that he'd "haul that buzzard's baggy hindquarters into court if his trash begins to veer so much as an inch over the legal line!" And Ray's face held such a blend of self-righteousness and suppressed violence that I'd felt I was seeing him clearly for the very first time—and not as I wanted to see him.

And it was just as I was standing beside my flowers, mulling all this over and over in my mind, that I heard that thrashing begin in the woods. I looked over my shoulder and glimpsed Ray. He was heading away from me, down toward the river, breaking a ragged path through our wild raspberry bushes, heedless of the thorns, the few ripe berries, and the white blooms that would soon be lush and red. Now ordinarily that kind of carelessness would have made me furious, but Ray's feet were pounding the dirt path by then, and I could see even at that distance how breathless he was, and that red stains from crushed berries spotted the legs of his trousers like blood.

I ran toward him into the sunlit woods, calling out, "Ray! Ray!" until I heard his voice panting back like an answer: "It's McMullen."

"Yes," I said, weakly, and already I knew how everything would be. Already McMullen had backed that God-forsaken pickup of his most of the way across his property. He was nearly down to our bank.

It seems as if Ray pulled me through the woods behind him, though he didn't touch me at all. It was my own left hand that clutched at the right sleeve of my sweater as we ran, my own fear that carried me. The sputtering noises of McMullen's engine became louder, and I saw the backward motion of the old truck inching along in a diagonal path toward the edge of our property, moving nearer and nearer to the river.

And in his dooryard—just beyond the ramshackle house—was that huge black dog. The thing stood on the roof of its dog house barking savagely as we came closer, then it lunged from the house and ran at Ray and me—ran snarling till its chain stopped the huge body with a jolt, stopping the waves of awful noise with that one choking gasp. It stopped Ray and me in our tracks too, nearly stopped my heart, though the creature started up barking again as we ran on.

McMullen's truck continued to inch backwards, so that it looked for all the world as if he intended to back the thing right down the three-foot embankment that marked the beginning of the natural floodbank. Ray and I were running along the lower edge of the bank by then, below the truck, when Ray lurched uphill.

"What in unholy hell do you aim to do, man?" Ray's words cut through the barking and the crunching and grinding noises with a higher-pitched sound that was oddly like glass breaking. And McMullen's dumb, amazed, whiskery chin appeared, turning toward me as he poked his head out the window of the truck, his heavy-lidded eyes searching for Ray. Then suddenly the back wheels of that truck were rolling right over the embankment. I swallowed a scream and backed away. McMullen's engine choked to a halt, and then came the ugly crunch of metal underparts cracking as the truck's back end slipped downward and fell right off.

Thank God the junk did not hit Ray as it pummelled madly from that ruined truckbed. It spread out with clanks and rattles and a final whooshing sigh across the clean bank beyond Ray's feet, and I myself saw

116

the first tiny rivulet of the Chena when it began to lap like an eager tongue at a rusted piece of tailpipe.

Ray's face, when he turned back to glance at me, was crumpled with pain and fury. Then he was up the small hummock of bank and pulling McMullen from what was left of the truck's cab.

"You've ruint my truck—" McMullen's voice formed the words in that amazed, feeble, slow way of his as Ray pulled and shook at the long, tall body that towered over him so. Ray's fingers sought McMullen's neck, and purple veins began to rise like welts just above the knot of Ray's fingers. For a second I thought of upholstery piping, of a pair of old '40s-style living room chairs with that kind of trim that I'd had in Ft. Worth, and suddenly we all seemed like characters in some awful slapstick joke.

Then I was up the hummock too, pulling at Ray's clenched body so that I could feel McMullen's long, light weight curling and twisting below us. And I remember that I was shocked by the scent of Ray's body— shocked that even here, his perspiration held that clean, dignified, soap-tamed smell I knew so well.

McMullen didn't fight back at all. His long arms just flailed and flapped, like wet rags in a breeze. But I was pummelling Ray's back with my fists, shouting, "Stop it, Ray! Stop!" And when he finally dropped his hands and turned to stare at me, Ray had a look on his face exactly like a sleepwalker's.

McMullen stared at me too, then backed off slightly rubbing his neck. He leaned back against the door of the truck—which was nearly off its hinges. His gray shirt was torn, his lower lip dripped blood, and his mouth hung slack and open. I felt my body just go old and heavy then, like so much dead weight; I felt

sick, the way McMullen and Ray both looked, and I
wanted only to be away from there, in Ft. Worth or
anywhere, done seeing and hearing that awful black
dog gone hoarse and the trash that lay everywhere on
this land like a curse—

"This river— This river—" Ray spoke the words
lamely, his left arm motioning toward the mass of
glistening water that was just beginning to catch the
first rays of the long, slow sunset. "By God, man,
couldn't you—" Then Ray's voice cracked and he
started to sob.

McMullen's eyes met mine for a second time, and
his knees seemed to buckle under him. He sat back on
his heels and squinted at me, at the river, then at Ray,
whilst all the while that dirty, long-fingered right hand
of his went scrubbing and scrubbing at his neck.

Ray turned and half-ran back toward our property.
He made small choking noises in his throat, and he
pushed at me when I came too close, and I remember
having one moment of perfect clear-headedness when
I thought: he'll sell the property. But I kept my eyes
fixed on the path, I swear it, not letting my sight find
the perfect wild symmetry of my flowerbeds—as if some
penance now should be mine.

Well, Ray did sell the property. One week later. I
was numb as I signed the papers, saying nothing at all
when he quit his accounting job and immediately
bought a small souvenir shop, sight unseen, in Valdez.

Just as the guidebooks say, Valdez is small and
lovely—the Switzerland of Alaska—but full of that
dank, wonderful smell of the sea. It has both rounded
and steep mountains, and many green or pale blue
lakes, and those huge, egg-like boulders that appear

everywhere. They're massive and curvaceous—immovable looking things like the toys of God. They often make me think of McMullen's wintry yard, the way a fresh fall of snow could transform those trash heaps to an absolute wonder. Although I'd never mention that to Ray—

Ray says there's a chaotic shape to the scenery here, and there is a harshness, a dampness to the climate. The summers are cool and rainy, the sky dark and heavy with its perpetual burden of clouds. I haven't even managed to plant the seeds from the packets of Iceland poppies that Teddy, my oldest girl, sent last spring—poppies being the one flower that might grow easily in this thin, rocky soil. Maybe I've lost my enthusiasm for gardening forever, though I hate to think of that. I do try to write cheery letters back to our children in Fairbanks once a week, feeling a bit like a liar when I do it. And this is our life now.

But the worst part is that when I watch Ray talking earnestly to a customer about trends in costume jewelry—or when I see him bend over the rock-polishing machine that he keeps in the back room of the shop—or those times when he leans upward into the bright circle of light over the table where he mounts polished Alaskan stones into our specially designed jewelry bases—then most of all, I guess—well, he looks to me like a stranger. Like a man I hardly know at all.

I have an old snapshot I keep in the pocket of my smock—one of those candy-striped smocks that you have to wear if you hope to look right standing behind the counter in a souvenir shop—? And anyway, I just take that photo out and turn it 'round and 'round in my hand, trying to look at Ray from one angle after another. He's standing on the bank of the Chena, and his face is intent and pure, staring out across the river as if there might be something perfect there, something only he can see. But, after a minute, I always put it back into my pocket, feeling guilty for no sensible reason at all. It's then that I wonder how much blame a person really should accept for things that came of their own accord. And I wonder how anybody but God can ever truly fix blame for some of the most final and important actions of all.

I think of that July evening then, of the last time I saw L. T. McMullen. I looked back over my shoulder towards the riverbank, just stopped trying to keep pace with Ray in the woods and looked back. I saw McMullen's narrow, humpy-looking body poised above the river, his back all flooded with red sunset and bent over the remains of that truck. And I swear that it was a beautiful sight when his long, flame-lit right hand lifted gently and slid again across the lean, curving strip of his neck.

About the Author

Jean Anderson lives in Fairbanks, Alaska, where she supplements her writing with teaching, reviewing, and editing. Her awards include an Individual Artist Fellowship in literature from the Alaska State Council on the Arts. She and her husband have two children.